NANNY FOR THE ALIEN PRIMAL

A SCIFI ROMANCE

ATHENA STORM

ATHENAVERSE PRESS

Sign up for Athena's newsletter!
Like my Athena Storm's Facebook Page!
Join the Athenaverse

BOOKS OF THE ATHENAVERSE

Intergalactic Fated Mates:

Nanny For the Alien King

Maid For Him

Reaper's Property:

Monster

Savage

Brute

'90s Nostalgia Fated Mates

My Boyfriend Is An Alien

My Hero is An Alien

My Neighbor Is An Alien

Reaper's Pet Series (An Athenaverse Collaboration with Zora Black):

Caged Mate

Caged Prey

Caged Toy

Caged Slayer

Caged Property

Caged Pearl

Caged Beauty

Caged Bride

Alien Tormentor's Plaything

Alien Soldier's Prisoner

Champions of Ataxia Series:

Brax

Tur

Phynn'ro

Gyn

Mates of the Kilgari (An Athenaverse Collaboration with Celia Kyle):

Rescued by the Alien Pirate

Treasured by the Alien Pirate

Warriors of the Alliance Series:

Yaal

Duric

DESCRIPTION

He may be a king, but I have the greatest rank possible. It's called being a mom.

One day I get a knock on my door.

It's the Drokan King.

Turns out that the two orphaned kids my best friend left behind when she died are royalty.

He says I need to bring them to the Palace. And I need to come be their nanny.

He'll pay me handsomely and ensure I live a life of privilege and comfort.

But there's something more.

I see a glint a hunger in his handsome alien face.

A stiffening of his muscular, ripped body.

I can tell he wants me to be around him.

That he sees me as his.

I can hear his thoughts.

He thinks I'm his fated mate.

I can sense his desire. It's thick. Strong.
I can almost touch it. Taste it.

Am I going to give in?
    Be a human in this alien's court.
    Care for his children and tend his home?
    I will...but he can't call me a maid or a nanny.
    He has to call me...

A Wife.

(*I'll also accept "Mother"*)*Author's Note: This is a completely standalone novel set in the Athenaverse. Even if you've never come into the Athenaverse, you'll be able to enjoy this science fiction romance that has no cliffhangers or cheating and guaranteed happily ever after!*

ONE

EVALIE

If I stare at the screen long enough, can I will a message to show up?

If that were at all possible, I think a dozen messages would've come through on my Misiv just now. Instead, the device stays blank. Empty. My only contact on the entire thing is "Lord", and he's not answering.

I hear a grumble and the sound of movement, and instinctively I look up from the pearly sheen of the Misiv. I've been taking care of my kids long enough that I'm attuned to their every move. And, since they're just getting over being two-year old hellions, I like to keep a close eye on them.

Yet Or and Tali are still sleeping, simply shifting in their dreams. They know I'm troubled these days, and they might even be a bit hungry. Neither of those things make for restful sleep, so I'm grateful they continue to slumber in the musty dark of our apartment.

My mind drifts to thinking of the first time I saw the twins, nearly three years ago now. They were such round, lumpy babies, especially in the muscular arms of the person I only know as Lord.

The Drokan nobleman had come to our door completely unannounced, practically shocking me and Mar to death. He stood there, all tall and golden skinned, his wings elegantly furled behind him. The Drokan was handsome all right, but that was hardly noticeable. What I saw first wasn't any of that — it was the deep sadness weighing on him.

He held the two squalling infants that I now know and love, and explained they were his children. His children — and my old friend's Lani's. She'd gone to the palace to work as a servant, never forgetting to send money home every tenday. However, I hadn't seen her in years.

Eagerly I'd asked where Lani was, shocked and delighted by the idea of a Drokan-human union. Were they getting married? Would she be coming home?

The nobleman's silence told me no, even before he did.

With sorrow, he told me Lani had died in childbirth. I'd barely had a chance to register the tears that prickled in my eyes, before he was begging me to care for his secret, half-human children. He promised to support them financially, as well as me and my mother.

I would've said yes if only for Lani's sake. But with the added promise of an actual income, well... when you're a human on Genesis, you learn to take what you can get, and not ask too many questions.

So what could I do but accept?

A whirlwind of information came at me then, in addition to the two heavy bundles of baby. They were introduced to me as Orelon and Talissa, and their father told me to call him simply 'Lord.' He gave me the Misiv I'm now sitting with, which at the time blew my mind. A crystal-powered personal communication device like this could fetch a steep price in my neighborhood.

For nearly three years, the wealthy and mysterious Lord visited regularly — well, if you can call once every two months regular for a father — and responded swiftly to any of my communications. When Tali sliced open her foot, he had a quiet but incredible doctor to us in less than an hour.

Now, though... it's been a month since I've heard from him. His last money order didn't appear two weeks ago. I'm good at making things stretch, but at this point, I'm running out of money to take care of the kids. I can only feed them instead of me and Mar for so long.

Not to mention, as Or grows, he draws more and more attention. Thank the stars Tali remains entirely human-looking, but that doesn't help how fast Or's Drokan characteristics are rising to the surface these days.

His skin, which I'd been able to pass off as tan, is gaining the shine that turns it to gold. His little horns are nudging through the skin of his head, and his wings are too big for me to hide under a human boy's shirt.

Just last week, someone refused to serve us because they noticed Or's gawky wings poking beneath the thin fabric of his jacket. I didn't try to fight it, I only hustled us off before we could draw any more attention. The thing is... unwanted attention is coming for us, whether we like it or not.

Humans don't like the Drokan much, given that the race controls most of the world's money and we control none of it. I can't blame my people for being angry about that. Constellations know, I've been infuriated by the horrible poverty of my neighbor almost every day since I was old enough to understand not everyone lives this way.

To take it out on a child, though? A boy not even three years old? That is a degree of rage I can't comprehend. It scares me. Just like the thought of hearing Or and Tali cry from the pain of empty bellies scares me.

Get it together, Evalie. Fear never helped anyone solve a problem.

I jerk myself back to the Misiv. For what feels like the millionth time, I compose yet another message to Lord. There's no reason not to, even as my hope that he'll reply dwindles to nearly nothing.

Please, I write. **Please answer me. We are still out of money for food. I can't keep these children on my own, you know that. If you don't send us some funds, your children are going to starve.**

I stare at the message. It has a combative tone, which I don't intend, but I leave it as it is. Being angry that Lord might have abandoned his children is a lot easier than considering the alternative.

That he CAN'T respond.

Even the thought of that makes me feel nauseous. I can only pray that the guy went on a trip or something and neglected to set up care for us while he was away.

That doesn't ring true, though. No matter how ashamed of his half-human children, Lord has always provided for them. He wouldn't disappear, which means the most likely answer is really, really bad.

Because if something has happened to the twins' mysterious Drokan father... we're in big, big trouble.

TWO

AVIRIX

One word, repeated many times on a single screen, is making me feel like I've been punched.

Children. Children?

I blink, thinking that maybe the grief is getting to me. I must be imagining the messages on my brother's Misiv. After all, it's taken me weeks to hack into it. One of my staff might've managed the task in a day or two, but I insisted on doing this myself.

I guess some part of me knew there would be sensitive information on Iziqon's Misiv. But children? That's a step too far — I'm hallucinating the worst case scenario.

Yet when I open my eyes, the words remain, indelible on the glowing screen.

If you don't send us some funds, your children are going to starve.

And that's only the most recent message. Several times a week for the past month, similar messages have come from the same unnamed account. Escalating in urgency, certainly, but even the very first and more relaxed one is crystal clear.

We haven't seen you in a while now. The twins miss you! Come see us when you can, the kids will be excited for some time with their father.

I can deny the truth right in front of me no longer.

My brother, Prince Iziqon of the Plains, has children.

Not only that, he stashed said children with what seems to be a human woman in one of the worst neighborhoods in Besiel. There are enough hints and details in these messages to tell me as much. What the woman's words can't tell me, however, is *why*.

Where did these children come from? What on earth was Iziqon thinking, hiding them away?

My brother and I haven't always seen eye to eye on matters of state, but I've always supported him in everything else. Did he actually think such an indiscretion would cause more trouble between us? Surely he didn't think a few illegitimate brats would ruin his reputation with the court.

If he'd asked, in an instant I would've helped him find a good noble family to place them in. A good noble family of *Drokans*, for that matter, rather than whatever human household he left them in.

Not that I have anything personal against humans — it's simply that Drokans and humans don't mix much, outside of economic arrangements. I would bet that two Drokan children get a lot of attention in a human neighborhood. Certainly, they must stand out.

This matters, because...?

My brain is devolving into irrelevant thoughts.

Annoyed with myself, I get up and stride to my balcony. I wish I could leave the hash of emotions in my chest behind, but they follow me out into the sunshine.

Chief among my feelings is confusion. I genuinely have no idea what could have motivated Iziqon to hide his own children in the last place anyone would think to look. In a dangerous place, no less.

On top of that is a shameful wash of anger. I'm angry at Iziqon for keeping his children secret from me, I'm angry at him for doing something inexplicable with them. I'm angry at him for dying.

Even though the person I should really be angry with is myself.

Once again, I think about how I never should have let Iziqon go with the team sent to deal with the Pilger rebellion. I knew it was risky, but he begged me to let him get his hands dirty for once. He made a compelling argument that a royal presence would send a message.

And it did. A message that we didn't intend. According to my spies, the rebels read the presence of a Prince in Pilger as essentially a declaration of war. So they made a desperate and unexpected attack on the government encampment. In the melee, Iziqon was killed.

Which is all my fault. I should have put my foot down. It was too volatile of a situation, as I well knew.

It doesn't matter anymore, what's done is done.

Right now, I have a bigger problem than wrestling with my past decisions, namely the existence of these children.

From the human's messages, it's clear that she's in need of financial assistance at the very least. I can't stand the idea of my own blood wanting for food. Or what if one of them gets injured, and there's no money for medical care?

I must retrieve my brother's children, immediately. I

don't know why he didn't keep them in the palace, but as of today they are known members of my family. I will house and care for them appropriately.

Returning back inside and heading to my desk, I reach for my own Misiv. I'm about to call for Ferrar, but I stop myself. While I know my butler could handle this very well on his own, something keeps me from passing off the task.

I know I shouldn't run my own errands. It doesn't befit me, as King of the Plains Drokan. However... I cannot think of this as an 'errand.' No matter what Iziqon's attitude to them is — *was,* I remind myself with a pang — they are my family.

Just like he was.

If these children are of my bloodline, then I'm going to fetch them myself. I want to meet the humans who've been caring for them, and I want to see how they've been living.

Living for the past three damn years.

"Frustration will get you nowhere, Avirix," I say to myself, out loud. "Focus on the solution."

It's a common refrain for me, and the reason I'm a King who gets things done. When I was younger, I could lose my foothold in a negotiation simply by losing my temper. I don't do that anymore, and it means I solve issues swiftly and well.

And what issue could be more important than rescuing royal children from whatever hellish corner of Besiel my brother stashed them in?

My mind made up, I straighten. For the first time since Iziqon's death, I feel an odd bubbling excitement low in my stomach.

I suppose it makes sense. Despite the circumstances, this is rather thrilling. After all, it isn't every day I get to meet new family members, for the very first time.

THREE

EVALIE

"Maybe I can reverse trace the number - find out where he lives?"

Do you really think he'd let you know that information?

Good point. "Maybe I can bargain for credit at the market? Maybe they will extend that to me? I've never been late on a payment before..."

In this economy? Unlikely.

Pace, pace, pace. There wasn't much room to do it but I was doing my best. Doggedly, I walk back and forth, cutting a path in front of the twins who play happily in the corner with a stick and a rock.

It amazes me, when I take the time to notice, how resourceful those two kids are. I only hope I can keep their minds off of their impending hunger so they can be free to live like real kids.

None of that was going to happen if I didn't find a solution - and quickly. The Misiv was still silent. Even looking at it causes my anxiety to fly through the roof. Where could he be? How could he leave his children in such a state of distress? I know he loves them - it was clear each time he visited - so what could have possibly changed?

I feel a hand on my arm. Stopping in my tracks, I catch my mother's eye.

"Maybe...it's time to sell the Misiv. It would fetch a pretty price. And it would hold us over for a while." Her voice and gaze are steady and I hated that I agreed with her. But what if the Lord *did* finally reach out? We have no other means of contact.

I couldn't let it go just yet.

"I hear you but I can't just yet. It will throw too much attention on us. Attention I've been trying to avoid." My eyes stray to Or's bumpy back, the wings lumpily (and badly) concealed. There wasn't much more I could do to keep that a secret much longer...

The pressure on my arm increases, ever so slightly. "Ev - I understand that. I really do. But that may be a luxury we have to forego. Starvation trumps all of that." Again, her look, steady and sure, bores into my face. I *know* she's right, but...

Uncharacteristically at a loss for words, we stare briefly at each other. A knock interrupts us and I move swiftly to answer it.

I immediately regret doing so.

The doorframe is obliterated by the menacing figure of Rrame - the local Skuyr gang leader (every shitty community has one, so I'm told). Before I can even greet him, he barges through and stands in the middle of the room, taking up most of the available space.

In the weak light of the lanterns, his silver scales appear dull and muted. His horns are chipped and unkempt, not surprising given that Rrame spends most of his time harassing the citizens of Genesis rather than focusing on personal hygiene.

"Can I help you with something, Rrame?" I ask, motioning to my mother to stay as close to the children as possible. I need as many barriers between him and them as possible.

"You could say that, yes. Word on the wind is that you, my attractive young thing, are in a bit of spot when it comes to money." His voice is too loud, too confident and altogether too out of place in this little hovel.

It may not be fancy, but we've lived here in harmony long enough, just the four of us. His brash and overbearing energy rankles the kids instantly. I see Or's face darken as he takes in the brute.

My eyes flit to the Misiv, which thankfully, is somewhat hidden from plain sight. "What do you mean?" I ask, trying to sound casual.

"I mean, that money is tight for you. Which means that food is scarce. Which means...grumpy kiddos. I think I can help you with that. Because I'm known for, uh....helping out, from time to time," he says, a smarmy smile bruising his jagged face.

Yeah. I'm sure you're known around here as a real people person...

"We're in a bit of a tight spot at the moment, but we're working it out," I reply, making a motion that he can leave now.

"You see, the way I look at," he says, dodging my gesture and insinuating himself even further into the room, "is that I can fix all your problems with one simple solution. Quick, easy, and everyone wins."

I swallow, knowing that I have to at least hear him out before I can reject whatever he is saying entirely. While I've never had need of his services in the past, I can only imagine what his 'terms' might be if you receive any help from him whatsoever.

"Simple. You're single. I'm single. I've got the means, you've got the beauty. You marry me, I take care of you and these uh...charges of yours and everyone wins. I'll even throw in some generosity for that mother of yours, the old bat."

My mother, with the patience of a saint, merely clears her throat in response. Rrame turns to face her.

"Oh, sorry about that. Didn't see you there. So...what do you say? I'd say it's a sweet deal. Hard to walk away."

My shock at this clunky and ridiculous proposal, combined with the fact that he's just insulted my mother renders me (for the second time today) speechless. It's then that I notice that the children have completely stopped playing and are listening to every word. Or has stood up and I can see his little hands balling into fists.

I'm not sure what he understands, but he seems to get the message that this situation is very, very wrong.

Several seconds tick by as Rrame examines my face and I try desperately to form my response. He is handsome, in a roguish, fractured sort of way, but something about him makes me shudder. Perhaps it is the stories of what he does to those who do not pay back what they owe on the heinous deals he strikes.

But there is no world where I could ever actually *marry* the man.

I open my mouth to speak. To politely decline. But the words don't come out. Instead, I hear, "Go 'way, nasty man."

Or's voice rings out, clear as phaser fire. Rrame's shit-eating grin stumbles and turns into a grimace.

"I apologize for that outburst, Rrame. They are a little grumpy. And, I'm flattered by your proposal, but I'm not in the market right now, so if it's okay with you..." I again try to usher him toward the door.

Can I even get this ass-hat out of my house?

"I don't think you understand the opportunity I'm offering here..." his voice has lost its conviviality and is now akin to how a snake would speak if it could talk.

"I'm well aware of the opportunity, as you put it, but I'm just not—"

"I said, GO AWAY!" Or repeats, his little foot stomping the floor.

Rrame's face drops all pretense of civility. He turns, slowly, to face the boy.

"I don't think this one knows how to speak to one's elders. Perhaps I should school him on it..."

He makes a move towards the boy.

"No!" I shriek. "Please, let's just sit and talk this through.."

No one must touch this boy. Not if I can help it.

Rrame does not turn to face me. That's a bad sign. I look to my mother, hoping to find something, *anything*, I could possibly use to fend off this angry gang leader when a knock shatters the silence.

It couldn't have been better timed.

FOUR

AVIRIX

It's the smell that hits me first. Wattle and dung and... desperation. Following the coordinates that align to the address on IziQon's Misiv, I find myself standing outside a ramshackle dwelling, mainly made out of found materials.

There has been an attempt at keeping it neat but it is a losing battle with the poverty and sadness that permeate the place. Whatever the inhabitants have done within, it cannot compete with the degradation all around it.

Knocking forcefully, I'm expecting to see frightened (and possibly toothless) humans dwelling within. So, I am flabbergasted when the door opens to reveal a human female that quite literally takes my breath away.

"Yes?" Her voice sings like a small bell, clear and bright. Her hair, a riot of reds and browns, falls languidly over her shoulders, framing piercing green eyes. She looks shocked to see me. It's a good thing, because it seems to distract her from my own reaction.

"Uh, yes. May I have a moment of your time? I am

looking to locate someone or...someones," I stammer, trying to keep my voice steady.

"Oh...of course," she replies and I swear I detect a note of relief in her voice. She steps aside and I enter the hovel.

Though it's clean (as much as it can be), I can't believe that people actually live under these conditions. The floor is packed dirt and the sparse furniture inside looks like an afterthought.

Inside, I encounter the oddest collection of people. A surly looking Skuyr dominates the room. Beyond him, a small older female stands, her eyes flitting from the floor to my face. Near her, two small children stand, but I can't make out much about them, as they are standing deep in the gloom. The light in the hovel is poor at best.

Before I can say anymore, the Skuyr sweeps past me. His hand grips the doorframe. Just before he leaves, he swings around to the gorgeous human female and says, "This isn't over," and leaves.

As he does so, I'm keenly aware that everyone around me lets out a breath I hadn't been aware they were holding.

I, on the other hand, am struck with an intense wave of hatred as the Skuyr walks past me. Before a few weeks ago, my feelings towards them ranged from indifferent to mildly annoyed. But now, knowing that they are responsible for my brother's death, I feel a rage that I was not expecting race through me.

Struggling to regain my composure, I turn back to face the woman. Her beautiful face, like a cool drink of water on a hot day, helps to bring me back to myself.

"To what," the older female says, "do we owe the honor of meeting you, Lord...?"

I decide to get straight to the point. Now, strangely, the

beauty of the younger female has become somewhat of a distraction to me and I need to focus.

"It appears you have been the primary caretakers of my younger brother's children. I am here to reclaim them."

To the point. Good.

At my words, the two small children that had been hiding in the shadows emerge. Their appearance stops me cold. The boy is the spitting image of his father. His body is dotted with the royal markings of his heritage and it's obvious he is of noble blood. The girl, however, takes me completely by surprise. She is, by all appearances, completely human.

It all suddenly clicks. That's why he hid them away. Their mother is human. It's the only explanation. And their mother must be this woman standing before him. That can be the only reason IziQon permitted them to live in such a horrible place. He always did have a softer heart than I.

The realization that my brother is dead rises up within me, almost as fresh as the moment I first heard it. With a sting that almost makes me gasp, I swallow sharply.

"Oh? Your brother? I did not know he had a brother," the young woman says, snaking her hands protectively over the shoulders of the twins who look at me warily. Their faces are living replicas of my brother and it suddenly hurts to breathe.

"Is that so? What did you know of him?" I can't quite believe this woman would know nothing of the father of her children.

"Not much. Just that he was a wealthy lord who provided for his children. Until...recently." Her head bows and I sense, despite her surroundings, that this woman has a deep-seated sense of pride.

But, pride or no pride, I won't have my niece and

nephew live one more moment in this hellish hovel. They must be taken to the palace immediately for proper care.

"Well, let me give you further information. I am King Avirix, of the Plains Drokan. My younger brother was Prince IziQon, second in line to the royal throne. Recently, he, unfortunately, met an untimely end. That may explain his absence and lack of response."

A thick cloud descends over all of us as the news sinks in. The young woman gasps and brings her hand to her mouth. The older female tuts softly and stands next to the younger woman, putting her hand on her shoulder. It is then that I see they are mother and daughter.

The children, meanwhile, have heard my words but look confused and pale. The import of what I have said doesn't quite resonate with them entirely.

"Oh, oh no, no, no, no, no..." the young woman intones, shaking her head as if that would shake the reality away.

"I'm afraid so. It's quite a blow to us all. I am sorry to bring you such news."

For some moments, I simply stand, letting the people before me absorb the message. I can't quite decide whether the young woman's reaction is appropriate or staid. It seems much too reserved a reaction for the death of the father of one's children, but I don't know the circumstances of their pairing, so I dare not speculate.

I clear my throat. Enough time has elapsed and I must be getting a move on.

"Well, yes. As I said, I'm sorry to deliver such news but now it's clear to me that we must move on, to respect his legacy and his...progeny."

The woman looks up, her jade green eyes brimming with silver tears.

"What....what does that mean?"

"It means the children must leave with me at once. To the palace. Where they belong."

For what seems the umpteenth time today, the air leaves the room.

FIVE

EVALIE

Wait, what?

There's more information coming my way than I know what to do with. I feel like someone just swatted a dozen balls at me and I'm trying to bounce them all back to the other side of a court all at the same time.

Rrame – and his creepy proposal. The father of the twins – dead. This Drokan before me – their uncle. And also the King of the Plains. And now he's taking them?

As I process all of this, I'm a little ashamed by a voice I hear calling out in my own mind. *What about me and Mar?* It asks. After all, through the kids, the Lord – IziQon, I guess – was also our lifeline. If the kids go, does that mean...

Also, who would have thought that this hot, forbidding nobleman in front of me is the King? How does a good-looking King end up in my shitty little home?

I look back toward Mar, trying to get my bearings. Just behind her, I spy Or and Tali. I guess that should be, *Prince* Or and *Princess* Tali.

As hard as this all is to believe, trying to picture the two of them dressed to the nines in royal palace clothing is perhaps the hardest. It actually makes my lip curl slightly in a bemused smile.

Then I hear the King tap something on a personal Misiv pad. Suddenly, two Drokan warriors who were apparently lurking outside barge into my home.

"Take the children," Avirix says. Just like that. Like they were furniture he'd just picked out.

Before I can move, the Drokan warriors break toward Mar. One reaches for Or, the other for Tali. The kids scream in protest. Or actually bites the hand of the one reaching for him. The warrior backs away.

"What are you doing?" the King asks.

"It bit me, my Lord."

"*It* has a name," I scowl.

The warrior ignores me and grabs Or by the back of the neck of his shirt. Or lets out a wail that Tali, already in the arms of the other warrior, matches.

"All right, stop," I shout. The authority in my own voice surprises me.

The guards look at Avirix. I note the concerned furrow of his brow. Probably disappointed this isn't as easy as he'd assumed it would be. He gives a curt nod to the guards, who drop the kids. They immediately run to me, one to each leg. Mar comes behind me and gently coaxes them into her own arms, leaving me to do...

What? I'm a poor human living in a hovel. What can I actually do or say to a King flanked by armed warriors?

"The kids aren't going anywhere without me," I say, my voice low.

Avirix starts to scoff, but the noise of dismissal gets lost in his throat as he stares at me and sees I'm serious.

If only he could hear my heart pounding and know how scared I am.

I hadn't really thought my gambit would pay off. Faced with the Drokan's silence, I'm not really sure what to say next. Fortunately, Mar adds something to the mix.

"The children have had enough loss, My Lord," she says softly, still cradling the kids. "Will you really take them away from Evalie, the only caretaker they've ever known?"

Another quick response seems to be forthcoming from Avirix. But again, he clamps his mouth on whatever Kingly retort he'd instinctively been about to offer. Instead, something flashes across his face. I think it's uncertainty.

There's something endearing about seeing a powerful royal display that kind of vulnerability. For a moment, I catch a glimpse of the person behind the royal title. What I see tugs at me.

Then it's gone, replaced once more by the serious, regal detachment.

"Fine," he says.

I almost don't process what he's said.

"Fine?" I ask.

"You may come. Too. You will be their paid nanny. I would need to hire one anyway. Now, we must leave."

It's my turn to have a comment catch in my throat. I'm speechless. On top of all the other things that have been thrown my way in the last few minutes, I really didn't expect *this.*

Did he just say I'm moving to the royal palace to continue caring for these kids as a paid nanny? What the hell kind of twist is *that?*

I'm about to agree to the deal and run to pack my things when I look and see Mar. Her eyes have widened in pleasant surprise. But I can see something else in them, as well. It makes me turn back to Avirix, who is already starting for the door.

"My mother must come, too," I say quickly.

"Must?" Avirix repeats, his voice dark. He stares at me.

"My Lord, may my mother join me... at... at the palace...?"

"No." It's a gruff, annoyed response.

Then, once again, I see his façade drop a moment as he considers me and Mar. Who is the man behind the mask? How do I get through to him?

"She may not come," Avirix says, but his tone has softened considerably. "However, rest assured you will be paid enough to take good care of your mother. That is my offer... Evalie."

The sound of my name in his voice makes my knees wobble. I don't give myself time to consider that, though. Avirix's demeanor makes it pretty clear that there's not a lot of time for me to consider the offer. Which *is* generous, all things considered.

I wish I could take Mar aside and talk all this over with her. What's in front of us is an incredible change. A reversal of fortunes, but knows what unexpected costs there might be? And Mar hasn't been on her own in ages.

But what's the alternative? Let Avirix take the children out of my life so I can go on to enjoy wedded bliss with that creep Rrame?

I lock eyes with my mother. I can tell that she can read in my eyes the thoughts that are racing through my head. She gives me a thin smile and a small nod, then pushes the children a few steps toward me.

Go, she's telling me, *I'll be all right.*

The decision's been made, I suppose. We're leaving and

going to the royal palace. It's not like there was ever really much choice to be made, I suppose.

After all, one doesn't really gainsay the King of the Plains.

SIX

AVIRIX

I was sitting in my study, yet I was acutely aware of exactly where in the palace the nursery was. Like having an itch on your back you can't reach. I couldn't do anything without being incredibly conscious of the fact that there, in the nursery, were two children and a human female.

My *brother's* two children. My niece and nephew. And that woman. Evalie. When her mother said her name back in the hovel, it had sounded to me like birdsong. Then, when I'd said it aloud to her, it had made me feel... giddy. As though the words themselves were like a laugh.

That is the most ridiculous, sentimental j'gar *dung you've ever thought,* I chastised myself.

There was so much to do, and here I was trying my hand at poetry over some human nanny. Important things needed my attention. My desk was stacked with communications and briefs that had to be addressed and responded to.

Including negotiations with the Skuyr rebels of Pilger.

That one had to be handled with the utmost care. Screwing up that up could lead to more death.

And, in turn, more orphans. Like my niece and nephew. And more widows. Like Evalie. Beautiful and sad Evalie whose name is like –

Stop it, you sick bastard. That's your dead brother's woman.

Shame immediately sunk my mood.

I tried to get more work done, but there was no use. I wanted to know how she and the kids were settling in. I considered sending a servant to go and look in on them, but that would only delay my knowing. It wasn't like I would get any more work done while waiting for news than I would if I just went down there myself.

Might as well scratch the itch.

A quick check-in, then back to work, I tell myself as I hurriedly slip away from my study. In quick time, I'm down several halls and a few flights of steps to the nursery. No doubt, the kids will be asleep and the nanny folding clothes or something like that. So I'll just peek in, satisfy my curiosity, and be gone in a moment.

Except what I find in the nursery is chaos.

When I open the door, it is to the sound of two children wailing. The girl is running around in circles, distraught. The boy is on the floor, his pants half-on and half-off while Evalie kneels before him offering him new pair after new pair, which he snatches from her then throws across the room.

I stand there agape until Evalie finally sees me and walks over with a quick bow.

"What is this?" I ask.

"This, my Lord? This is two children distraught at having been suddenly uprooted from the only home they've ever known, into a huge, unfamiliar palace with clothing and toys and beds that are not theirs."

"Are you saying they'd rather be back in –" I stop myself short of saying *that shithole you lived in* and instead finish with, "back in their old place?"

"I'm saying, My Lord, that this is all new to them," Evalie says. I respect her tactfulness. "Also, they're hungry," she adds.

"Well feed them," I say.

"The cupboards are bare," she says.

"The cupboards...?" It takes me a moment to process what she's saying. I wonder if I've hired an idiot. "Why didn't you just call for their dinner?"

"I did try to find the kitchen, My Lord. But the palace is too big. I got lost just looking for the stairs."

I'm not sure *I* could even find the kitchen, I thought, but that's what we have Misivs and the servants for.

"Didn't you try to call the servants?" I ask. I can see her looking confused. "With the Misiv?" I ask further.

She looks around the room, clearly looking for some awkward, bulky Misiv like the old model she had in her house. I try not to sigh as I go to the wall by the doors. I run my hand over a small, clear strip on the wall at about chest height. Immediately, a tiny panel opens, revealing the inter-palace Misiv.

"Wha...?" Evalie says, her mouth agape. She wanders over to me, staring at the Misiv the whole time, like she's just found a treasure. Her amazement is endearing. "You mean," she says slowly, "I can just come over to this thing and *order food*? Right from here?"

I demonstrate how to call up a servant and request that dinner be sent to the nursery. Evalie continues to stare at the thing like it's a miracle. Then, she runs her hand over the clear strip on the wall and the panel slides back into place, hiding the Misiv once more.

"So cool," she says.

I chuckle in spite of myself. Her wonderment is adorable.

"You're making fun of me, My Lord," she says.

I immediately feel a bout of regret.

"No, no, no," I assure her.

"I am just a poor human. I don't know how things work in a palace."

"That's all right, I assure her. Besides, there is plenty of time to get to know. No one is going anywhere any time soon."

That seems to reassure her. There is a quiet moment between us. I ought to go. There is much work to do. I've checked in, I've offered a helping hand. Why am I lingering?

"Thank you, My Lord, for showing me how to use the Misiv," Evalie says, "I'm sure you have much to do."

"Yes. Yes. I do." I should go. Yet I don't want to. "Of course, I also feel I ought to get to know the children. I... don't even know their names."

"Would you like a proper introduction?" she offers.

"Please."

I follow Evalie over to the kids. Clearly interested in my and Evalie's interaction, they've stationed themselves together on the floor. The boy's clothing is still all askew. The girl sucks a thumb and holds his hand.

"My Lord," Evalie begins, "this is Orelon and Talissa."

"A pleasure to meet you," I say.

"Kids, this is King Avirix."

"*Uncle* Avirix," I say. I kneel down before them. "Your father was my brother. Just like he's your brother," I say to the girl. Then, I reach out toward the boy. "Here. Let's finish getting you dressed," I say softly.

Which is when the boy – Orelon – bites my hand and the girl – Talissa – begins to scream again. Evalie chastises them, embarrassed, and I try to pass it all off as good-natured fun.

Then I spend the next twenty minutes trying to get to know them. It goes no better. Finally, the food arrives from the kitchen and I excuse myself.

I hurry back to my study, feeling as though I've scratched an itch at the expense of stubbing my toe.

SEVEN

EVALIE

Thirty two paces. That's how many steps it takes to cross the widest part of the nursery suite. Compared with the nine paces back at my dwelling, it feels downright luxurious.

And yet...

Even thirty two paces can feel stifling when they are the only thirty two paces you can make. And right now, they are the only ones I feel comfortable making. But, oh, how I wish I could venture beyond these nursery walls.

No doubt the children do as well. But after the disastrous kitchen hunt yesterday, I dare not take them outside what is now familiar...and, now, utterly boring.

The palace, though, is overwhelming. Not just for me but for the children as well. I see their eyes widen and glass over when they try to take in the magnitude of the place, the endless hallways, the plush furnishings and the ostentatious decor.

Even I have a problem taking it all in. I can't imagine what they must be feeling having never seen anything like it before.

Still, I'm getting to the point where I'd give my right arm to find somewhere else to play. We are all getting restless.

I wish I had a map of the palace...or a guide. Although everyone we have encountered is polite enough, there is a frost there. The only real connection of any kind is the damn King himself and it's not like he's going to take time out of his busy day of...I dunno, running a kingdom, to escort us around.

But, he was very kind last night.

As I pace, I am forced to concede that yes, he was very kind last night. But I can hardly expect him to continue with such kindnesses and displays of attention. He has so much more to do.

Is boredom and loneliness the only reason you want to see him again?

Once again, I have to force myself to admit what I know to be true. I don't exactly mind his attentions, not only because it's a chance to get to know this palace better, but because...well, he's very easy on the eyes. And he's kind. And he's regal. And he's...unlike anyone I've ever met before.

That's enough reasons. Leave off for now.

Suddenly, I feel a tug at my sleeve. Looking down, I see Tali's giant eyes looking back at me.

"Booorrrrreeed," she intones, drilling the sound into me.

You and me both, sister.

I scruff her hair.

"I know, sweetie. I am too. But this palace is scary. Remember? We need to figure out how to get around first."

"Out! I want out!" Or chimes in, jumping and stamping

his feet. He is less subtle than his sister but, again, I can't say I blame him.

"Soon, Or, I promise."

"Now!" Stamp, stamp.

"Hey, is that anyway to get what you want? How about we talk about something else?"

Both twins cock their head to the side at the exact same time. No matter how many times they do this, it always feels like a magic trick to me. I hope I never tire of it.

"What," Or says, not quite giving me the satisfaction of asking it as a question.

"Isn't this place beautiful? Aren't you so glad to be here?" I gesture around us at the beautiful and spacious nursery suite. I'm not sure how much they understand of their recent change of address but maybe talking about it will kill at least a few of the unending minutes between now and nap time.

"Why?" Tali asks. At least she asked me an actual question.

"Well, your uncle, who is now your protector, decided that it would be best if you had the best food, the best beds and the best care possible. So, he took you home to where you belong."

For a brief second, both children look closely at their surroundings as if assessing the truth of my statement. Everything around them is new and gorgeous - clean and bright. Everything I couldn't give them back home.

I fool myself, just for a second, into thinking that this might assuage their wanderlust (and perhaps my own). That they may suddenly become content with the room around them and we can settle into an easy day ahead.

Who are you kidding? Are you content to sit here all day?

I'm not sure if they read this thought on my face or they

just make their own conclusions, but they quickly dismiss any wonder they may have nursed.

"Booorrrrreeedddd," Tali intones once more.

So much for that...

Sighing, I put my hands on my hips.

"All right. You win. Let's go for a walk."

They immediately, like small dogs, go into conniptions of joy - yipping and jumping.

I put up a finger to stop them.

"Uh-uh. Not like that, we don't. If we are to be in a palace, we must act like we belong in one. Now, follow me."

With exaggerated steps and sticking my nose in the air, I adopt what I believe to be a royal stance and begin marching to the door of the nursery.

The twins, eager to do anything, quickly fall into line behind me, mimicking me clumsily. But at least they are quiet and finally - finally - distracted.

Opening the door, the hallway spills out before me in two directions, a dizzying array of doors dotting the walls. It baffles me that behind each door is yet *another* room. What could one family possibly need all these rooms for?

A small flare of panic arises in me and I find myself breathing deeply to squelch it.

Just take it one door at a time. Maybe set a goal.

The idea tamps the flare down - just a bit.

"All right, my royal ones. We will march to the first five doors we see. Each royal hand must touch the royal door, otherwise, it will no longer belong to us. Do we think we can do that? Remember, it is your sacred duty."

My solemn words and demeanor cause the twins to likewise become stolid and grave. Or's forehead wrinkles in stoic concentration and Tali bites her top lip to keep from smiling.

Setting a slow pace, I step out in the hallway and make a big show of processing, regally, to the first door on the left. With my best royal impression, I brush the door languidly, as if knighting it.

The twins soon follow. With each door, my panic abates a little and I start to see that the hallway is nothing more than that - a means to an end. Perhaps, with time, I will learn it after all.

Our royal procession marches on.

EIGHT

AVIRIX

"Let us all be assured that everyone has the best interests of trade and clean commerce at heart. All will be well!"

My voice rings out through the dining chamber. For a split second, even I believe it. I sound like I spoke with authority and with finality.

And finality is what I crave right now. This lunch has been the most ponderous affair I've had to sit through in many months. And, given how dull daily royal life can be sometimes, that is saying something.

Still, it had to be done and it had to be said. And, at least right now, I think that everyone is satisfied - for now. The lunch had brought together my advisors and the merchants recently affected by the rebellions at Pilger. The ensuing chaos had caused major shipping delays, cutting into the only bottom line these merchants cared about: money.

But, through sheer will and compromising grunt work, we had been able to assuage them from their most heated demands and impress upon them that everyone would be back in prime shipping speed soon.

The merchants stiffly and slowly make their way towards the exit. I indulge in a tiny bit of hope that I might actually be able to leave this stuffy room and get some fresh air - maybe even get some real work done.

Wishful thinking...

"I don't wish to contradict the work we have accomplished today," a voice rang out, "but we will fail ourselves and our...constituents if we do not do something about the... unfortunate events in Pilgar. This meeting has solved nothing."

This is exactly what I was hoping to avoid. He couldn't leave well enough alone. Why I would expect him to is beyond me, but still. After working for so many hours to talk the merchants down from taking up arms (or worse still, assembling their own militias), he is, once again, stirring the pot.

Grall. An advisor for so many years, I've lost count. And my most conservative. He's a holdover from the previous king and so entrenched in Drokan that not even I wanted to force his ouster.

But, at every turn, he presents the most conservative, and dare I say it, brutal view on things. Now, for instance, he would like nothing more than to crush the rebels of Pilgar beneath his booted feet.

"It has solved *enough* for my liking," I reply, calmly as I can. His eyes catch mine and I sense the tension of the assembled advisors, servants and merchants that are still, as if caught in amber, all around us.

This kind of alpha male sparring is not new to us, Grall and I, but, as the rebellions have increased and his rhetoric has become more violent, the disagreements have mounted. I feel, at times, that I barely have control of the situation.

The peace I've offered the merchants is tenuous but

steady at the moment. Grall knows this and it chafes at him. But, he dare not openly flout his king.

So, after a few tense seconds, he grunts and sweeps from the chamber, his scepter and breastplate clanking angrily. With his exit, the rest of the merchants and advisors also leave, movement and speech slowly returning to them.

Blissfully, I find myself alone for a few seconds to regroup. Strangely, though, I find my thoughts wandering back to Evalie and the kids. What might they be doing right now? I hope Evalie is using the Misiv I provided to tour the palace.

But isn't it all too much? From the look on their faces the past few days, I can tell the palace and all it entails seem a little overwhelming. After seeing where they live, I can only imagine what the change must be like for them.

Perhaps I should have provided a tour? As a child, I recalled how imposing the palace could be - and I was born into such luxury.

Enough musing. Get back to work.

Shaking my head, I gather myself and leave the chamber, heading towards my private offices.

Just then, however, I hear screeches that I have never heard before. Or at least in these halls.

Children. I distinctly hear the sound of children. It sounds so incongruous after spending an afternoon with dry, old men's voices, all resembling the sound of leaves crunching.

Turning my head, I see a small trio far up ahead of me. They are facing away from me but they are unmissable - it is the children with the beautiful and mysterious Evalie.

Though I squash it immediately, a strange flutter erupts deep within my chest.

Just happiness that the meeting is finally over...

But, I have to admit, I'm intrigued. Besides, a little diversion couldn't hurt.

Stretching my long legs, I decide to join them. As I approach, however, I am struck by the game they are playing.

In a mock-solemn procession, they move from door to door, placing their little hands upon them, as if knighting each one. I hear their chattering voices guessing as to what lies beyond each door. After a few moments, they move on, satisfied that their guesses (completely ridiculous) are perfectly right.

It's not unlike a game I played as a child with IziQon. We often got lost in the palace and made up many stories as what lay behind each set of doors we encountered. It became so entrenched with us that often it wasn't until adulthood I knew what was actually behind the doors - so imaginative were our own speculations.

Smiling to myself, I start to close the distance between us when the giggling suddenly stops, as if someone stoppered all the air.

Turning a corner, I see them, frozen in a sad tableau. Their faces line up in one direction - that of a large portrait hanging in the center of the wall.

IziQon. One of many of his portraits throughout the palace. Still, I had forgotten this one was so close to the nursery. What a foolish error not to have had it moved elsewhere.

Their voices snake up to me.

"Who that?" Orelon asks, gruffly. He seems intrigued, even if he doesn't know why, like there is a connection there he hasn't quite made yet.

"Father," Talissa says, grimly. She has caught on faster than her brother.

Both children turn to Evalie for confirmation.

"You're right. It must be him. It looks just like him."

I can hear the crack in her voice as she stares at the painting. The children, without being aware of it, draw closer to her.

"He was a good man. Never, ever forget that. He loved you both so much."

Evalie bends to embrace both the children as they continue to stare ahead at the painting.

Her lover. Of course, she grieves.

Any thought of joining them, of sharing in their mirth, evaporates from me. Now, I feel foolish for even thinking I could be part of their levity.

In full retreat, I silently back away down the hallway until I can turn and head swiftly to my office.

Only a fool would think a woman would be ready to move on so soon.

But move on to what?

NINE
EVALIE

The sound of tiny snores reaches my ears, and I smile with relief. Tali and Or are sleeping like rocks. Little, snoring, rocks.

It's a welcome change from the first night here, when I couldn't get them to settle. I couldn't get myself to settle, for that matter. Strange surroundings don't exactly make for restful sleep.

Yet today, I clearly wore them out. Between the palace exploration AND finally finding one of the huge gardens to play in, the twins had plenty of exercise — both mental and physical. I'm oddly proud of myself, even though that seems silly. I've been entertaining and caring for these little people for nearly 3 years! Why does today feel like a special success?

Because this situation is crazy, that's why.

I've been so worried about the kids acclimating, that I haven't thought about how this whole massive change is affecting me. I certainly feel a lot of relief knowing that Or and Tali won't starve, but I remain a little overwhelmed. And I miss Mar.

I straighten, suddenly full of conviction. After all that's happened, I deserve a break, and a bit of time to myself. If going for a walk alone in our dingy neighborhood calms me, then a walk in this palace's incredible gardens will definitely do the same. Fresh air always settles me.

Now that I know how the room's big Misiv works, it's a piece of cake to set it to alert mode. If the twins wake up or call for me, the room's Misiv will send an urgent messages directly to my personal Misiv.

Which... is weird to think about that way. Before, I always thought about it as Lord's Misiv. Since he's gone, though, it has become completely mine. I never thought I'd be the kind of person who could afford a personal Misiv.

You can't. It was a gift, just like living in this palace is a gift. A TEMPORARY one.

Sighing at my own ability to bring myself back to earth every time, I head out the door. Navigating the snaking hallways by memory is challenging, but I make it to the garden with only one false turn delaying me.

The huge sprawling grounds are even more beautiful at night than they were this afternoon. Sure, the bright colors of some of the flowers don't pop the way they did in the sunlight, but I like the muted tones of the night better. Everything looks otherworldly underneath a nearly full moon.

I wander along the pathways, breathing in the heady scent of night-blooming vine flowers. The air is balmy, caressing my face with the gentlest breezes. It's paradise.

As soon as I think that, I begin to notice the other luxurious touches beyond the plants. There, a fountain with trickling clear water. Here, a bench wrought from a shining and flawless metal — with more such seats scattered through the garden.

In front of me, a fruit-bearing tree I don't recognize, with fallen fruit beginning to rot on the grass. The smell of the turning fruit is sweet enough for now, yet it still turns my stomach.

Humans all over Genesis — humans in *my* neighborhood — go hungry every day. We have to boil our cloudy water just in case. And here, in this place, food goes bad on the ground and clear water exists for aesthetic pleasure only.

If Lord — Prince Iziqon — lived with this much wealth... surely he could have helped us more. He could've cared for the community that he placed his children in, not just solely the kids' needs.

The inequity is galling to me. The cost of that gleaming table and chairs under the arbor to my right could probably feed twenty families for a month, if not more. I was fond enough of the Prince, but seeing where he came from I can't deny that I don't understand him. Why turn his gaze away from poverty he'd seen firsthand?

So lost in my thoughts am I that when I turned the corner of a tall hedge, I squeak at the sight of a tall silhouette. I'm startled to find anyone else here, which is ridiculous. It's not *that* late at night!

At my noise of surprise, the silhouette turns into the moonlight, and I see — it's King Avirix. A cauldron of excitement and nerves bubbles in my stomach immediately.

"I'm so sorry for disturbing you," I stammer, on the verge of turning and leaving.

"Oh, no need," Avirix replies, in that deep rich voice of his. "I was simply thinking of my brother, which is typical of me these days. I find my mind turning to him at every opportunity."

"I see," I say hesitantly. Grief seems like a pretty private thing, but maybe Avirix doesn't want to be alone with it right now?

Before I can say anything else, Avirix continues.

"I apologize for not saying so earlier, but I'm so sorry for your loss." He dips his head. "I should not have let my grief for my brother blind me to yours."

"Oh — no — not at all." I cock my head, confused by his words. "Indeed I'm sorry for *your* loss, my King. He was your brother. This cannot be easy for you."

"Yes," says Avirix, his face puzzled. "But it cannot be easy for you either. After all, he was the father of your children."

Taken utterly aback, I freeze. My mind runs through every time I've talked with Avirix, and I realize at no point did I clarify that the Prince asked me to take the kids. The King doesn't know about Lani. And why would he?

"The twins are not my children," I tell him, trying to keep my explanation simple. "They are the children of your brother and an old friend of mine who went to work as a palace servant. When she died in childbirth, Avirix brought them to me."

"Orelon and Talissa are not yours," repeats Avirix slowly, like his brain can't quite comprehend what I've told him. "My brother's lover was someone else — was a palace servant?"

"Exactly." I nod encouragingly. "The twins's mother's name was Lani."

Avirix lifts eyes to me that are still full of a surprise, but also something else. There's a strange satisfaction behind his gaze, almost like he's pleased by this information.

I don't know what that means, but I do know he's staring at me intently. My heart flutters as I regard him steadily back.

Why does this revelation matter to him?

My heart thumps in my chest as I inadvertently lock eyes with Evalie.

Can she tell how thrilled I am to hear that she wasn't involved with my brother?

I strive to wipe any hint of that from my expression. She's just explained to me that my niece and nephew are orphans. They've never known their mother and barely knew their father. This is a heavy and sad truth, but I'm self-ishly caught up in my own relief.

Which is ridiculous. It's not like I'm going to pursue anything with Evalie, even knowing now that she isn't akin to a grieving widow. It's merely helpful that I don't have to feel so uncomfortable about my undeniable attraction to her.

That's all.

"My brother never told me about the children," I say finally, needing to break the growing silence between us. "So of course I didn't know of the relationship that produced them. I'm sorry for making an assumption."

"Too many apologies between us already." Evalie waves

her hand. "You don't need to say sorry for thinking what anyone would in this situation."

"I appreciate your understanding." I incline my head, even as my words come out more stiffly that I intended.

Why does THIS human female make me so awkward? I'm a KING, for Krodo's sake.

"Were you and Prince Iziqon not very close, then?" Evalie asks the question curiously, but then blushes so hard I can see the color in her cheeks even in the moonlight. "Oh, I shouldn't pry, I'm—"

"Not sorry, surely. Too many apologies, didn't you say?" I interrupt her with a smile, and am rewarded with an astonishingly sweet and sheepish one in return. "And I don't consider that prying, although it is a more complicated answer than you might anticipate."

"Isn't family always complicated?" returns Evalie, wryly. She is no longer flustered, with that elegant calm descending onto her beautiful features once more.

"True," I acknowledge. "And I suppose my story with my brother is not unusual. We were very close as boys, practically joined at the hip. But when I took the throne and began aggressively changing some of my father's policies, well... there were tensions."

"Did Prince Iziqon disagree with you?" Evalie's lovely face is open, guilelessly curious. I feel like my heart is loosening, talking to her about my departed brother. I haven't had much of a conversation with anyone about him, since he died.

"That was part of it," I muse, half to myself. "At times he agreed with my principles and not my execution. At other times he felt I was disrespecting our father. I never got the sense that he was jealous of me, exactly. More that he wanted to be able to prove himself, too."

As I say it, I realize that is precisely why Iziqon wanted to go to Pilger so badly. If I had understood my younger brother better sooner, maybe I could have offered him a way to find purpose here in Besiel. A high-level post, a domain of affairs all his own...

But it's too late for that now.

"Did you know my brother well?" I ask Evalie abruptly, needing to stave off the impending wave of guilt. I can tell the question takes her off guard, but she covers it well.

"I didn't." A half-smile twists her mouth, as her gaze focuses beyond me, on the garden. "I had no idea he was royalty, for one thing. And I couldn't tell you much about his personality apart from the fact that he loved his children. He was good with Or and Tali, they always enjoyed his visits. But..."

She hesitates, and then closes her mouth. Her eyes flick back to my face and I see a guardedness in them I didn't expect.

"Please, continue." I spread my hands out. "Perhaps you have questions about Iziqon?"

Evalie shifts from side to side, hardly enough to notice. But I do. Somehow in just this brief exchange, I've become attuned to her every motion.

"If you're concerned about saying something you shouldn't, know that I'm aware my brother kept many secrets. You may tell me the truth."

"Well, it's not exactly a secret of his... or maybe it is." Evalie straightens, and I see a touch of determination come into her vivid green eyes. "It's more of a question about him, as you said, although you may not know. Why did he hide his children in such an impoverished neighborhood?"

"I have asked myself that many times since I found you

and the little ones," I reply softly, remembering the day not so long ago that I finally hacked into Iziqon's Misiv.

"Was his reputation so important to him, that he refused to keep the kids at the palace? And why would he send money enough to feed and clothe Or and Tali, but entirely ignore their surroundings?"

I gape at Evalie. She's saying so much of what I've been wondering myself — but she's not done.

"The children were provided for, I'm not saying they weren't. But they grew up surrounded by misery. Iziqon grew up surrounded by THIS!" She flings her arm out to indicate the lush garden. Her tone has grown heated, and I don't know what to make of it.

"I agree with you that Iziqon's decision to place them in a human sector is puzzling," I venture.

"AND it makes no sense why he would do that, and then refuse to help the neighborhood he left them in. He has *so* much wealth — a tiny corner of this palace could improve the lives of my community *permanently*. But Iziqon couldn't be bothered. He could use us to hide the kids he was ashamed, but he never thought to think that we might deserve better."

I stare at Evalie. She stops, flushed again. Her shoulders are heaving slightly with the passion of her speech.

And I? I have no idea what to feel.

This human female has just insulted my brother, and implied that the inequity in the Plains is somehow the fault of my family having a palace that befits our station. However... she's also asked questions that continue to be akin to my own.

Was Iziqon more hard-hearted than I ever knew?

That thought rocks me. It feels desperately disloyal, and

mingled with the horrible guilt I pushed away earlier, well. I can hardly bear it.

"You'll have to excuse me," I hear myself saying brusquely. My words bristle with offended displeasure. "I am not used to hearing my family being so roundly disparaged. I will not listen to another word."

Without waiting for a response from Evalie, I stalk off.

And feel strange and unsettled for the rest of the night.

ELEVEN

EVALIE

The kids are occupied in the playroom, so I take a moment to step out on a balcony and try to clear my thoughts.

The view of the Plains is breathtaking, but it does little to distract me. It's crazy how quickly one becomes accustomed to things. Three days ago, if you'd told me I'd quickly get bored by the sight of the vastness of the Plains kingdom from a balcony in the palace, I'd have laughed in your face. Yet, here I am, unable to be impressed enough to wean myself off the thoughts that have been cycling through my brain all morning.

I was so stupid last night.

Here's a great idea, Evalie, insult the deceased brother of your current benefactor who also happens to be the King.

What the hell was I thinking?

You know what you were thinking.

I grimace at my own obviousness. What I was thinking was that here was a chance to get to know Avirix. I was thinking that by sharing my truest thoughts, I'd get him to reveal what he hides behind that mask of his.

Stupid, stupid.

Stupid to talk human politics with the Drokan King. Stupid to talk about his dead brother. And, stupidest of all, letting yourself develop a crush on the freaking King of the Plains! It doesn't matter how hot he is, or how nice his rumbly voice sounds. It doesn't matter that I've seen glimpses of something real and vulnerable in him.

And even if he was interested back, which he obviously could never be, but even if he was... a human and Drokan relationship can only end in one way.

A brief image of a robed, hooded Avirix delivering their children to some hovel flashes through my mind. It brings me both pleasure and pain. Pleasure at the silly idea of partnering with Avirix. Pain at the knowledge of what would follow such a partnering.

Even if you don't die in childbirth, you'll be kept hidden. Any family would be discarded. How does that sit with your crush?

Unfortunately, the feelings I had seemed unabated, even in the face of grim reality.

"Human woman! We have found you!" says a deep yet thin voice behind me.

"Surrender in the name of the Drokan!" another follows, less thin but also not as deep.

"Shh! *I'm* the talker," says the first voice in a poor attempt at a whisper.

"I can talk, too," says the second voice in its natural soprano.

"Nuh-uh."

"Uh-huh."

I turn around, hands high.

"Please! I'm innocent," I declare in my best frightened voice.

Or and Tali are behind me. Or is on Tali's shoulders and they've thrown a long robe over themselves to look like one adult-sized guard. Or has a very serious face on. Tali keeps peeking through the opening in the robe at me.

"Wait a moment," I say, playing up my suspicions. "I don't think you're a Drokan guard at all."

"Yuh-huh," Or says in his natural voice. Then, he quickly recovers and in his best baritone adds, "I mean, yes we are."

"Let me see your wings."

Or peeks down into the robe.

"Wings, wings!" he hisses.

"Wings!" Tali says from within the robe. Then, she reaches out through two holes they've cut in the sides of the robe and she lets fall two towels, holding them more like sails than wings. She does her best to flap them.

This movement unsteadies Or. Before he can topple over, I rush forward and grab him, swooping him up in my arms.

"Help! The human is attacking me!"

"You'll never get me," I cry out. Then, I throw him on the bed and start ticking him. Tali jumps into the fray and starts tickling him, too.

"Wait!" Or says to his sister between laughs. "You're on... my side...!"

Finally, we all collapse into different corners of the bed with a sigh.

"You two..." I mutter.

"We saw you were sad," Or says.

"Why are you sad?" asks Tali.

"I'm not sad."

"Something's wrong," Or says. He's always been the more perceptive of the two.

"I just have a lot on my mind."

"Is it because of our daddy?" Tali asks.

"No, stilly, it's because of the King. Our uncle," Or says. Like I said, perceptive.

"Are we gonna have to move again?" asks Tali.

"No," I assure her quickly.

"I wouldn't mind going home," Or adds.

"This is home now," I say. *At least, I think it is. Assuming Avirix doesn't have me fired or deported for what I said last night. I haven't heard from him all day so far. That's got to be a good sign, right? If he were angry, I'd know.*

The kids' mood has changed. Their attempts to cheer me up have now led to their own dour state.

"Who's hungry for lunch?" I ask in an excited voice. The idea of lunch stirs them a little. "How about a little kirsh and gush?" I suggest. It's their favorite noodle and sauce dish. Mar was excellent at making it. I just hope the sophisticated cooks in the kitchen don't balk at making such a peasant's dish.

"Yeah!" the kids call out in unison.

I hop off the bed and hurry to the Misiv. I run my hand over the clear strip on the wall and just as I'm about to order, an incoming message pops up on the screen.

Evalie. You and the children's presence are requested at lunch with his majesty, King Avirix. Be ready in ten minutes. A guard will escort you through the palace. Please respond with receipt of misiv.

I send back a receipt reply, stating that of course I and the children will attend.

But I'm freaking out. I'd hoped to get through the day without hearing from him. That would mean I was off the hook, right?

Is Avirix going to fire me, now? He surely can't actually

want to just eat lunch with us, right? This is some sort of ruse. Has to be.

Keep it together, Evalie.

"Change of plans, kids," I announce, trying to keep any tension out of my voice. "Dress up nice. We're going to be having lunch with the King."

Neither of them move.

"C'mon, c'mon. This'll be fun! We've never dined with royalty before."

"Will we still be able to have kirsh and gush?" Or asks.

"Well... we'll see," I say. "Hurry up. We don't have a lot of time."

The kids rush off to get into something nice. I run through the possible scenarios of what's to come. If he tries to send us away, or me away, I'll fall on my knees and beg his forgiveness.

I stand by everything I said the night before.

But I guess I'm in the game of politics, now. A little white lie might be in order.

TWELVE

AVIRIX

I stare at the table, set for four for lunch, and consider cancelling the whole thing. Why am I doing this? I can just imagine my advisors' reactions if they knew what I was doing. They would claim I'm 'debasing myself before this human servant'. They would remind me that once I am wed and have children of my own, these children of my brother's will be but several rungs down the ladder of inheritors of the throne. Nothing more.

Yet I couldn't get Evalie's accusations from last night out of my head. I went to sleep with my mind full of defensive remarks. Then woke up with her accusations still fresh in my mind and my defenses sounding false to my own inner ears.

Then there is the situation of the children. I recall my own frustration and confusion at IziQon's having left them in a human slum. There had been something noble about his commitment to providing for them. But that was all he had done. Provided for them. Not *cared* for them.

Now, it seems, I was falling into the same trap. Yet

instead of being miles away in another town, they were mere steps away.

I needed to change all of that. Respond to Evalie's points in a more understanding way. And start trying to find a means of connecting with my niece and nephew. With Orelon and Talissa.

So I had cancelled a medium-important luncheon with a trade union representative and opted for this family meal. There'd be hell to pay when some of my advisors found out. Hell to pay for a King, of course. Which is more annoyance than anything else. One of the perks of the job.

There is a knock, then a servant opens a door at the far end of the hall. Evalie and the twins walk in. I notice that all three have dressed themselves up for the occasion. For the twins, that mostly means shirts and pants that match and are buttoned correctly.

For Evalie, that means a cream-colored matching tunic and flowing pants with red piping. The clothes flow around her body while also giving hints at the perfect frame beneath the thin fabric.

I clear my throat and gather my senses. I'm about to speak when they stop a few feet from me. They're all very formal and stiff. Which makes me start to feel formal and stiff in turn.

"Thank you," I say, "for joining me for lunch."

"We... thank my Lord for the... kind... invitation," Evalie says haltingly, clearly trying to strike some sort of ceremonious tone with me. It's quite a different pose than the one she took last night. I wonder if she's worried about how things fell out between us.

I want to broach the subject with her, but it doesn't feel like the right moment. Instead, I crouch down and speak to the children.

"You both look very nice," I say.

"This itches," Orelon tells me, pulling at the tight, high collar of his shirt.

"Mine, too," Talissa says, tanking at the fabric around her crotch.

"Sometimes," I say in what I hope sounds like a conspiratorial whisper, "my formal clothes itch, too."

"Then why do you wear them? It's stupid," the boy tells me.

"This *place* is stupid," Talissa joins in.

"This lunch is probably going to be stupid," Orelon one-ups her.

"Children, stop that. King Avirix is being generous of his time and –"

"We don't care," Orelon whines, and buries his face in her leg.

Talissa continues to tug at her pants while staring straight at me. It's unnerving.

"We want kirsh and gush," she tells me.

"No," I say, involuntarily scowling at the thought of that mush. "We will be having boiled *agione* for an appetizer, followed by –"

"Perhaps," Evalie says, reacting to the faces the kids are now making, "we don't need to run through the menu. My Lord. Why don't we just sit down. Everyone is hungry."

"Yes. Of course."

Evalie leads the children to the table. I stand by the chair set for her and as she gets to it, I pull it out for her.

"Oh. Thank you, My Lord."

"Please, no more of that. And... please allow me to apologize for last night. I coaxed you to speak truthfully and then got mad when you did as I asked. That was unkind of me. And ungentlemanly."

Evalie pauses, half-seated, half not. I can see she's about to make some obligatory protest. The kind one feels one must make when a King declares himself to have been wrong. It's the last thing I want from her.

"Moreover," I go on before she can say anything, "you were right."

"I. Well. Thank you. My Lord. My King. Avirix. King Avirix. Thanks. To you." Watching her fumble out that adorable reply makes my heart pound a little harder. I see her flush, an endearing human trait that only serves to win me over to her even more. Then, she hurriedly sits in her seat which I push in for her.

I am suddenly feeling much better about everything. Then I sit down and see the scowls on the children's faces. Out of the corner of my eye, I see Evalie note my displeasure at their displeasure.

"You know," she says loudly in an almost sing-song tone, "I was nearly arrested by a Drokan guard this morning."

"You were – what?" I ask, suddenly concerned.

"Oh yes," she says, but for some reason there's humor in her voice, not alarm. "It was very scary."

I hear the children snickering at their end of the table. It starts to click.

"How very upsetting," I say in my most extreme 'kingly' voice. "I must have words with that guard. He should be punished to the fullest extent of the law."

"Oh, that won't be necessary," Evalie says. "I dealt with the situation."

"No, no, I insist on discipline among my troops," I say. "It's possible I know the rogue." At that, I look across the table accusingly at the twins. "Aha!" I shout and bang the table.

They start, then bust out laughing. I give Evalie a thankful look. She smiles, then leans toward me.

"If winning them over is part of the point of this meal," she says astutely, "then I might suggest your cook learn very quickly how to make kirsh and gush."

I nod in another show of gratitude. I hop out of my seat and poke my head into the kitchen. The chef's face falls when she hears my commands. Nevertheless, she says nothing, and a few minutes later two piping hot bowls of the mushy food are in front of the twins.

Another perk of being King.

THIRTEEN

EVALIE

Lunch is actually going OK. Which is better than I could have expected. I'm not fired. He actually acknowledged my points. And now he's engaged in more-or-less pleasant conversation with the twins while they shovel forkfuls of kirsh and gush into their mouths.

I'll be damned, I think. I'm halfway through my main course – a cold *ogapi* salad that tastes more delicious than just about anything I've ever had in my life – when I let myself finally relax.

Avirix has managed to get the kids to say more than three words in response to some of his questions. I can tell they're starting to get bored, however. Avirix is trying to amuse them with an anecdote about when he first became king. I'm enjoying it but the twins are past the point of being able to sit still and listen to anything, however funny.

Praying that the kids just mind their manners, I keep my focus on Avirix and his story. I try to ignore the mild shuffling I hear coming from the twins' side of the table. *They'll settle down. He's almost done his story. Then we can excuse ourselves and...*

I hear the *splat* just an instant before Avirix pauses mid-word.

Looking toward the twins, I see a bit of gush dripping down Or's face. Tali's fork-turned-catapult is still in its 'fire' position. The gush drops off of Or's chin and plops in a gooey spill onto the immaculately clean table linen.

Ah crap...

Or pauses a moment, then starts to laugh. He sticks a finger in the trail of cheesy goo from the gush and makes a big deal of sucking his finger dry. Tali laughs, too. Which is when she gets a face-full of food, as well. Or's hand is a sticky mess from his flinging the food at his sister. He makes a point of rubbing the stuff off on his sister's shirt.

Crapcrapcrap...

Suddenly, the two kids are standing in their chairs and flinging food around at each other. Or is the first to expand the battlefield, ducking under the table and emerging between me and the King. Tali grabs some left-over dipping sauce from our appetizer and hurls it our direction.

It splatters right in Avirix's face. I swear I can see the congealing sauce start to boil from the red rage that fills his eyes.

Then Or reaches into my salad and smears dressing on my cheek. He laughs hysterically. And I take a chance.

Grabbing some bread from the table, I suddenly pull the neck of Or's shirt wide and stuff the bread in there, then smash is against his chest.

Or writhes and wriggles.

Avirix makes a barking sound. At first it scares us all. Then we realize he's laughing. Me and the twins all exchange looks. I'm surprised. They're delighted.

The food fight is on.

Avirix has terrific aim and soon the kids' lovely formal wear is stained from his assaults. My own hair is quickly sticky with lunch and a bit of dessert, too. Alliances are formed and quickly broken, resulting in new truces that last about as long as it takes someone to rush back to the table and re-arm.

We're all having a wonderful time when the door to the hall slams open. A severe-looking Drokan, bearing an official's scepter and a breastplate indicating his advisory rank, barges in on our play.

"What is going on here?" he bellows. His voice has a cringe-inducing, birdlike squawking quality to it. It matches his features. "My King!"

Avirix pauses, mid-hurl of a bit of pudding. He stares at the advisor but says nothing.

"Where are the servants?" the advisor demands, seemingly of the air. Suddenly, as if summoned from the ether, several appear. "Clean this mess up and get his majesty some new clothes!"

Avirix actually seems chastened by this buzzkill. He wipes his hands on a napkin and approaches the ambassador. Some heated words are exchanged. I actually can't believe this jerk gets away with giving Avirix that kind of attitude. Eventually, Avirix seems to summon some of his kingly demeanor and the advisor gives way. He slithers out of the chambers.

As Avirix returns to the table, I note the servants at work.

"Excuse me, children," I say, getting the twins' attention. "What do we do with our messes?"

"But *they're* doing it," Tali says, gesturing at the servants on their knees.

"I'm sorry," I say with a note of offense in my voice. "What is the rule?"

"*Always* clean up our mess," the two say dutifully in unison.

"We had our fun, now we have a responsibility," I say. I gesture for them to get going and soon they're joining the servants in helping clean up.

I find something moderately clean to use to get the gunk out of my hair. As I do so, I watch Avirix stare in horror at the kids on their knees. Some of the servants don't seem to know what to make of the children, either.

Right. Royalty probably isn't supposed to do such thing, I think. I watch Avirix, wondering if he's going to demand they stop. It seems like he's about to, but then he quiets himself and just wonders at the kids willingly helping the servants.

I sidle around to him and offer him the clean end of the napkin I was just using. He takes it and looks at me, his face still quizzical.

"I've tried to make a point about teaching the kids to accept the consequences for their actions," I explain.

Avirix nods thoughtfully. But says nothing.

For the love of stars, I think as he absently wipes at some of the food on his clothes, *why is this man so hard to read?*

Avirix leaves before the children and servants are done cleaning. I usher them back to the nursery and try to ignore the stares from the palace folk we pass.

I give the kids a good bath, then take a quick shower myself. I clean the food off myself, marveling at the places it managed to reach. For a split second, I have a fantasy of Avirix in the shower, cleaning his own body off. I wonder where the food ended up on him.

Perhaps I could help him clean up, I think.

Stop that, I immediately tell myself.

I hurriedly finish in the shower and get myself dressed and out into the nursery. There's no good that can come from thoughts like that.

Just be glad you didn't get yourself fired today and call it a win.

FOURTEEN

AVIRIX

A few days after the food-fight lunch, I'm wishing I had some kirsh and gush to launch at the two Drokan seated across from me.

One is Grall, looking as miserable as always. The other is General Prix. Grall's brought him to my study to try and convince me to change course on Pilger.

"We look weak, Your Majesty," Prix says.

"He speaks the truth, Sire," Grall adds.

"It is called diplomacy," I remind them. "And we are negotiating from a position of strength."

"Are we, My Lord?" Prix asks.

His attitude is dangerously close to insubordination. I consider calling him out on it. Then choose to remain quiet. *Let him have his say, vent his frustrations,* I think.

"The rebellion must be crushed."

"What would you do, General?"

"Burn Pilger to the ground." Prix bites back something else, considers, then decides to say it. "It is how your father would have responded, My Lord."

Now I really do want to call out Prix's attitude.

Invoking my father like that to try and get a response out of me. I temper my emotions, refuse to give him the pleasure.

"My father might have. Probably would have. But I will not."

Prix and Grall exchange looks. I wonder how long they've been cooking up this little plan of theirs to try and convince me of engaging Pilger militarily. The thought of them conniving in some dark room in my palace pisses me off.

"We're done here. Dismissed. Both of you."

His discipline kicking in, Prix immediately rises and bows. Grall is slower on the draw, but eventually leaves me alone.

I sigh and rub at my temples. What a shit day. I wish this hadn't been the last meeting of the day. I was exhausted going into it. But Prix's insolence and Grall's scheming have me all keyed up. With nowhere to go.

Then an idea occurs to me. I quickly summon Ferrar and give him a few hasty commands. He hurries off to fulfil my wishes and I make a dash for the nursery. They shouldn't have gotten dinner, yet, if my timing is right.

I've been getting to know their schedule these last few days. When my schedule allows, I've been stopping by and collecting them all for dinner. Evalie and I have been trying to teach the children which silverware to use for which course. Talissa seems to enjoy the formality of it. Orelon stubbornly refuses to listen.

I kind of like that about him. It brings back happy memories of IziQon's own defiant streak.

Evalie rises quickly as I enter the nursery. I note a smile on her face. I think it's a smile indicating she's happy to see me. I like that smile.

"Oh, hello," she says. "Kids, it's your uncle."

In a sign of how close we're getting, the kids actually greet me.

"What's for dinner?" Or asks quickly.

"And how many courses?" asks Talissa, showing me how she can count on her fingers. She gets 'three' and 'four' mixed up, but still manages to get to 'five'.

"Follow me and we'll find out," I say. Then I turn on my heel and head into the hall.

In a moment, they've all caught up to me. Then, confident in their ability to navigate the palace now, the twins pull slightly ahead of me. So they're unaware at first when I bank right instead of the usual left toward the dining hall.

"Hey, wait!" Orelon calls out.

"Catch up, kids," I call back.

They do, then stumble over themselves as they stare up at me in confusion. I try to suppress my grin. Evalie sees it, however, and her eyes light up at my mischievousness. The light in her eye makes it even harder to maintain my serious charade.

Eventually, we come to a set of doors that I push open, revealing the garden. And in the middle of the paved patio before us sits a fully-set dinner table. It's piled high with food. All around the patio, hover candles float and flicker, powered by tiny energy crystals.

"Whoa," Orelon whispers.

"Pretty!" Talissa sings.

"Oh my," Evalie sighs.

All three reactions please me enormously.

"Is this for us?" asks Talissa.

"Absolutely," I say. "Go on. Grab a seat."

The kids both hesitate. Despite the progress I've made gaining their trust since the food fight, they're still somewhat wary of me. They glance from me to Evalie, who

NANNY FOR THE ALIEN PRIMAL   67

encourages them forward. Given confidence by her approval, they hurry for the table. Immediately, their fingers are in the bowls and plates, then in their mouths.

Evalie and I hang back a moment, watching them.

"This is quite beautiful," Evalie says softly.

"I'm glad you like it."

"What was the inspiration behind it?" she asks. There's a hedge to the question, as though she is wary of prying.

I think of my agitation with Prix and Grall. And how I feel none of that with Evalie.

"I had a trying day," I confess to Evalie.

"Then why...?" Evalie starts, confused. "Surely you don't need a burden such as a garden dinner with us. If you... had a difficult day."

"I might have thought the same thing a few days ago," I tell her. "Only now... being around the twins... and you... actually helps me to relax."

"Oh my," Evalie says with a small laugh.

"What?" I ask, suddenly concerned.

"If *we* help you to relax, then you really *must* have had a rough day."

I laugh and nod. Then I gesture toward the table and she and I make our way to it, joining the twins. Evalie forces them to sit down and act somewhat civilized. I shoot them little 'party-pooper' glances behind Evalie's back. They seem to enjoy that.

Then we are all eating and laughing. The stresses of the day begin to fade like the light of the setting sun. Twilight descends and I can imagine that my kingdom is one of peace. That the pleasantness I'm finding in this patio extends all across my land.

The twins act silly and Evalie balances indulging them

with trying not to have them make her look bad in front of me. It's all delightful.

Yet something dark gnaws at me, even in the midst of this joy.

I shoo the thought away and try to just enjoy the moment. After all, a King deserves to relax now and again. Perhaps a garden dinner with his nephew, niece and their nanny is not what my father would have done with his time off.

But, as I reminded Prix and Grall, I am not my father. This is my life. My enjoyment.

So why is it that some part of me wonders just how long this idyl can really last?

FIFTEEN

EVALIE

I'm feeling drunk, and I haven't had any alcohol. It's more the heady effect of this garden-set dinner. The scent in the air from the flowers. The decadent food. The beautiful, floating candles. The soft evening breeze.

The company.

It all combines to make me feel lightheaded. Not in a dizzy way. Just that wonderful, slight-buzz feeling that makes everything feel like it's contributing to your happiness. At one point, as we eat, I even find myself leaning toward Avirix, seated beside me.

I catch myself just in time. I pretend I dropped something between our chairs and am just reaching to pick it up. I even go through the charade of 'grabbing' at nothing and 'putting' it on my plate.

Don't read into this, I tell myself. *This is just Avirix playing the part of the fond uncle. The kids need this. That's what this is about, Evalie. The kids. He's not hanging around to spend time with you.*

What he's doing is paying off, too. The kids may play at

being stubborn when he's actually around, but I can tell they look forward to seeing him in the evenings.

So do I.

I'm settled back in my seat, feeling delightfully full, when I see Tali start rubbing at her eyes. Or, who is chasing some bugs, yawns mid-grasp for one.

"It's getting late," I say, forcing myself up. "I should get the kids to bed."

"Oh. Yes. Of course," Avirix says. He stands and the napkin in his lap starts to fall to the ground. We reach for it at the same time and both grab hold of it. I look up and find myself staring right into his eyes.

Something explodes.

Not metaphorically. Something actually has blown up elsewhere on the grounds. The ground shakes beneath us. I see the danger of it register on the king's face. For some reason, that's more unsettling to me than the boom of the explosion itself.

"Kids!" I call out, whirling away from Avirix. The twins come running, unsure, and I sweep them into my arms.

The rumble of the explosion fades and we can start to hear voices shouting. The breeze carries the smell of smoke and something worse through the garden.

Avirix looks up from his Misiv. "The perimeter has been breached."

My stomach drops. I feel myself go cold. *How is that possible?* I'm wondering, even as I try to think of where the safest place for the kids might be.

A guard is suddenly running into the garden, the soles of his boots clacking against the slate walk.

"My Lord! We are under attack!" the breathless soldier calls out.

"Who?" Avirix practically growls.

"Pilger rebels."

Avirix lets out a string of swear words unlike any I've ever heard in my life. I actually cover the twins' ears. Then the King of the Plains looks down at us.

"Stay. Put." The two words are commands that broke no disagreement or even an attempt at one.

I wouldn't know where to go, anyway.

Without another word, Avirix dashes off, outracing his guard to go and deal with the situation.

Situation? I think. *This is an 'attack'!*

Which means Avirix is running into danger.

"Evalie...?" Tali says my name softly, fear in her voice. Or is shaking in my arms. I can see him starting to get upset. They're confused, and all they know is that suddenly their nanny and their uncle are acting strangely.

"Hey, hey," I say, trying to keep the tremor of my fear out of my voice. "Everything's going to be OK. Let's sing a song."

I go into a melody they both enjoy. Or, perhaps more desperate to feel safe than his sister, joins in immediately. Tali eventually joins us on the first chorus. We finish the song and I lead them over to a stone bench. The tree behind the bench has low hanging branches that I'm hoping will offer some cover. In case we need it.

Y'know, from the freaking rebels.

I plop Or on my lap and bring Tali to sit close at my side. We end the song in a poor attempt at harmony. But they're settling down.

"What should we sing next?" I ask them.

"Where is Uncle Avirix?" Or asks me.

"He had to go take care of something, sweetly."

"That man said we're under attack," Tali points out.

"It'll be OK," I say. What else can I tell them? "You're worried about your uncle, huh?"

Or shrugs, but I can see the concern in his eyes. Tali, more straightforward, simply nods, sucking on her thumb.

"Have you grown fond of him, then?" I ask.

Another shrug. Another nod.

"Do you want to know a secret?" I bring all three of our heads together. "I'm fond of him, too."

"We know," Tali says with a giggle.

"You do?"

"Uh-huh," Or confirms.

"Well, what do you know?"

I'm glad to have the kids giggling. I kiss the tops of their heads, feeling a little relief myself.

Then the shadows move.

"Or. Tali." I say their names in barely a whisper.

They follow my lead as I climb over the back of the stone bench and try to push back into the shadows.

Out of the plants and trees, several Skuyr slip into the clearing of the garden. The orange flames of the floating candles reflect off their silvery skin. That is, what skin isn't covered in battle armor.

They mutter to themselves and begin to fan out across the garden. One of the Skuyr passes by the leftovers on the dinner table. He sticks his hand in a bowl and takes a bite of food. The beast chews with his mouth open as his eyes scan the garden for us, his other hand holding his blaster level.

The twins shake in fear beside me. Over the pounding of my heart, I can hear their shaking upsetting the leaves around us. I pull them close, hoping to keep them still and quiet. Or is about to start crying and I have to cover his mouth with my hand. It breaks my heart. But better that than having these Skuyr rip our hearts *out*.

The infiltrators gather not six feet from us and confer in whispers. There is some shaking of heads.

They can't find us. We're going to be OK, I think.

They turn to head back toward the palace. Then, one of them stops. Turns.

And looks right at me.

SIXTEEN
AVIRIX

Reports are coming to me fast and furious.

I stand near the front entrance of the palace. Smoke from the perimeter breach about a hundred feet to the north billows around me, blown by the wind. The Skuyr breached a weak point, then sent the majority of their force toward the main entrance.

It wasn't a good idea. My palace warriors had disposed with most of the Skuyr scum by the time I'd arrived. They'd left me a few to help take out. Which I did with grim pleasure.

How dare they attack my *home*?

My warriors responded quickly and efficiently. The Skuyr barely penetrated anywhere. The palace staff were quick to enact all emergency protocols, ensuring that no non-military personnel were in harms' way.

By all indications, this was a poorly thought-out attack. Which means we got lucky.

"Do you see, My Lord?" a birdish voice says behind me. Grall. Already eager to use this assault to forward his agenda. "The Skuyr of Pilger understand one thing."

"By the apparent strategy of this attack," I say without looking at him, "they understand nothing."

"This cannot go unanswered, Sire," says General Prix. He's toeing at the body of a dead Skuyrl. Probably searching for some trophy or token he can take off the corpse. Prix is great at his job. Too good. His mind is well-suited to the brutal nature of war. Which makes me uncomfortable to be around him. "A message must be sent."

"A message *will* be sent," I tell him. "Via Misiv. I will not allow them to escalate this fight."

Grall and Prix are both about to protest when suddenly I hear a shout from above me. I look up and see a servant half-out of the window and gesturing to the east.

"They've breached the garden!" the servant cries.

The twins. Evalie.

"Go, go!" I shout at several of the warriors nearest to me. They take off into the palace. I almost follow, then make a shift. The front lawn shares a very tall wall with part of the garden. I race toward that wall.

Letting my wings unfurl, I leap. With two quick flaps, I'm over the wall and quickly landing in the far edge of the garden. I've barely touched down when I let my wings retract and start running toward where I left Evalie and the twins.

Where I told them to stay!

If something has happened to them... I don't allow myself to finish the thought. Nonetheless, my heart is gripped by an icy hand. My stomach is in knots. I have never been so scared in my life. Even going into my first battle.

I leave the paved walkway and race through the plants and trees, taking a more direct route to our dining spot. When I burst out of the leaves, I'm confronted by a scene nearly as bad as my deepest fears.

Three Skuyr stand near the upended dinner table. One of them has the children in his grasp. A second one, female, holds Evalie's arms while the third one prepares to plunge a blade into her chest.

Instead, the third one looks down in shock as my vi-blade pierces straight through him from behind. His throat makes a sickly gurgling sound as he goes down, taking my weapon with him, stuck in his flesh.

The female Skuyr, shocked, lets go of Evalie. I reach out for Evalie to pull her away. My large Drokan fingers wrap around her thin, human wrist.

The minute our flesh touches, something happens. Time stops. The battle seems to vanish. I am no longer in the middle of a fight in the garden. I am –

I am relaxed and calm. I am in a future time. I am settled. Happy. I am surrounded by joy and growth. I am in love, and I am confident because that love is returned to me as passionately as I offer it. I am –

I am back in the garden. As quickly as the flash of emotions came, it's gone, and I'm once again pulling Evalie away from the female Skuyr. The Skuyr, meanwhile, has recovered from her shock at my attack. She leaps at me, her blade slashing down.

Reaching up, I grab her wrists and yank hard. I flip her onto her side, wrestle the blade away and slice it deep across her neck. She dies even as I turn to the third Skuyr. The one holding the twins. The one who is now the locus of all my royal ire.

"Stay back, King!" the Skuyr has the gall to hiss at me.

"You dare?" I ask, my teeth clenched. All my anger is seething over. Anger at this attack on my home and my people. Anger at the threat posed to Evalie and the twins. Anger at the passing of whatever blissful flash of feelings I just experienced. "You dare threaten me in my own palace?"

Before the bastard can answer, I hurl the blade in my hand at him. It splits his skull in two before burying itself in the tree behind him.

The body hasn't even hit the ground before the children rush forward and into Evalie's arms. They have been quiet up to this moment. But once they are in her safe embrace, they both begin to cry.

Suddenly, I find myself on my knees, my own arms embracing the three of them. I didn't even realize I was doing it. I'm just suddenly part of the group hug. I nearly pull away. But then Orelon squirms an arm out of the scrum to wrap it as far as he can around me.

The rage of the fight seeps away instantly. I am nothing, now, but a shield of affection for them.

"You're all right," I assure them, speaking into the mass of us. "You'll always be all right as long as I am around. I swear it." The words surprise me as much as they do the kids.

I hear my guards rushing into the garden. Their footsteps come up short as they see the destruction my rescue wrought. One tries to inquire after me. I ignore her and focus instead on the children.

Four pairs of large, round eyes look up at me.

"You... you promise?" Or asks.

"With all my heart. You will always be safe. All of you." I sweep my glance across them so that it also encompasses Evalie.

At the same time, I marvel at myself. At the forceful truth of the words I have just spoken.

How did these children and their caretaker become so important to me?

SEVENTEEN

EVALIE

I feel like I've been flattened.

The Skuyr attack really shook me up, to the extent that I didn't sleep. Every time I tried to close my eyes I saw those silver-scaled rebels seizing Or and Tali. Nothing worked to calm my racing mind last night, and nothing is working today.

I want my mother.

Plain and simple, I want Mar. Being around her can soothe me like nothing else. Moreover, if I died yesterday, she would've *never* forgiven me.

Luckily, at least Or and Tali are resilient. They're sitting in front of me, shoveling breakfast into their faces with their usual appetites. I'm sure nightmares will crop up in the future, but for now, the twins are fine. Unlike me.

Which Avirix somehow notices as soon as he walks in the door.

"Good morning Orelon, good morning Talissa," he says, patting Or on the head and ruffling Tali's hair. "How are you this morning?"

They wave the spoons I'd managed to jam into their little fists in the air.

"Goob," manages Or, grinning with a mouth full of *anarle*.

"Awake," replies Tali crisply, with a shrug before she goes for more *anarle* herself.

"That's good, that's good," mutters Avirix, his gaze now entirely trained on me. "And Evalie, how are you?"

I think about lying. I think about faking a smile and saying I'm fine, just a bit tired. Yet something stops me. Partly it's that I need Mar, but partly it's that I don't think Avirix would want me to lie to him.

"I'm still pretty rattled from yesterday," I admit, and watch as Avirix's face grows solemn. "I... miss my mother."

"Oh. Of course you do." Avirix takes a seat near me, and leans in towards me. He seems like he's going to take my hands, but then he doesn't.

"May I go visit her sometime in the next few days?" I rub the back of my head with my hand, hating to have to ask so soon in my time as official nanny for the twins. "I..."

"You..." prompts Avirix gently. The kindness I see in his eyes frees me, and the words come flooding out.

"I hate the idea that I might have died without saying goodbye to Mar — my mother," I confess. "And I can't stop thinking about the moment the rebels seized the children." I jerk my head at the twins, not wanting to say their names and get their attention. "I just... want to see my mother's face. It'll help me."

"Then you shall see her." Avirix nods thoughtfully, then stands up. "I shall make arrangements for you to have the afternoon off. I'll make sure the children are cared for, and I'll summon an escort and Convei for your trip to your mother's."

"Oh no, you don't have to do all that." I flap my hands in front of me, stunned by Avirix's immediate generosity. "I can wait til tomorrow, or the next day."

"It sounds like seeing your mother will ease you." Avirix sends me a soft, understanding smile that makes my heart turn over. "Why would we delay that?"

"Well... thank you, then. But no escort and Convei," I add hastily. "Those things will draw way too much attention in my neighborhood."

Avirix looks unconvinced for a second, but finally he bows.

"As you request," he tells me. "I shall find a caretaker for the children for the hours between lunch and dinner, if that is acceptable?"

"More than acceptable," I tell him fervently. "Thank you so, so much."

The rest of the day passes in a blur. It's second nature to me at this point to feed the kids, get them cleaned up and dressed, and do it all over again. They also seem to pick up that I'm not at my best, and quietly entertain themselves for the morning.

As Avirix promised, a competent Drokan servant shows up right after lunch and takes the kids well in hand. In a matter of moments, I'm out the door and walking to the nearest Buzz pick-up.

Naturally, it's a long walk. The battered old Buzzes don't pick up anywhere near the palace. And then, it takes what feels like a million stops before we get to my neighborhood. I find myself half-wishing I'd taken Avirix up on his offer of a Convei.

But a personal Convei, where I'm from? No way. Only the very, *very* wealthy have those. It would cause a damn riot in my streets.

Yet the whole tiring journey is worth it the moment Mar opens the door to our home. Her face lights up and I burst into tears and she gathers me into her arms. She's got her edges, my mother, but when it counts she's nothing but love.

I tell her everything that's happened, and she strokes my hair like she did when I was a little girl. I can feel the tension left by the Skuyr attack leaving me, even though Mar is eventually shocked by my story about it.

"The Skuyr rebels breached the palace grounds?" Her face contorts in surprised disapproval. "What good is all that money if those idiot royals can't keep a bunch of rag-tag fighters out of their fancy house?"

That forces a laugh out of me. Mar has correctly decided that my personal crisis is over, and is reverting to her usual self.

"I had that thought too. But they rebuffed the attack and Avixir... he saved us," I finish simply. "There wasn't a scratch on Or or Tali's head."

"Well what about your head?" demands Mar.

"He rescued me first. I mean, I was the one in immediate danger of impalement but yeah. Not a scratch on me either."

"Hmmm." Mar narrows her eyes. "Look my girl, I didn't want to interrupt and say this earlier, when you needed only comfort. But now you've settled down and I have to tell you — it's clear as day that you're fond of this King."

"I am," I agree lightly, trying to ignore the swooping in my belly. "He's good to the children."

"Don't try to fool me, Evalie." Mar crosses her arms over her stomach. "You've got some kind of moon-eyed crush on him, and it's not a good idea. You know that."

"Okay, okay." I bite my lip. "I'm attracted to him, and I enjoy his company. But come on, Mar, you raised me. Do you really think I'm stupid enough to think the King of the Plains and I could date?"

"... No," concedes Mar. "But be careful with your heart, Evalie. Drokan men use up and throw away human females, we've seen it plenty of times before."

"They're not the only ones," I mutter, Rrame's slimy face flashing into my head.

"True enough. I gotta tell you though, the bastard you're thinking of right now hasn't given up."

"What?" Startled more by the news than my mother once again reading my mind, I send her a worried look.

"Rrame has continued to stop by, and let me tell you he's none too pleased to find you still gone." Mar's eyes flash. "Entitled son-of-a-bitch."

"That's not good." I squeeze my hands together. "Mar, he's trouble. He might hurt you."

"Oh he won't, I'm fine, it's fine, I just thought you should know." Mar waves her hands. "Now stop worrying about me, and tell me more about Or and Tali. Does anyone ever make 'em kirsh and gush up there in that gaudy old palace?"

EIGHTEEN

AVIRIX

I leap off my balcony and into the air. Unfurling my wings, I catch a gust of wind blowing in exactly the direction I want to go.

Except, it isn't a direction I ever thought I *would* want to go.

I'm going to the monastery of the Reiders, to see if I can find a priest to talk with me. As I flap my wings and propel myself towards Moon's Brother Lake, I feel stupid yet again.

What am I doing, going to see a REIDER?

The sect is an old one, but that doesn't bring much respect to it. Most worldly Drokan, myself included, tend to scoff at the mystical ideas of the Reiders. The few worshippers I've run into are embarrassingly earnest, going on about life energy and a web of light we cannot see.

It's true that I can't see Krodo the Shaper, but our creator is a lot easier to believe in than an invisible glowing web.

Still, I'm stretching my wings on my way to a Reider monastery all the same. It all comes down to what I found last night. I couldn't sleep, so I wandered into the library and did some research on the flash of orientation I felt when I touched Evalie.

It was frustrating going, since I had no idea where to look. I wondered if it had something to do with a Drokan and a human touching, or was maybe some kind of hallucination based in my fear that Evalie and the kids would be harmed.

Eventually, I'd gotten to myths and spirituality. In one of those books, I'd come across this quote from a Reider priest hundreds of years ago.

"It is not given to any but the Reiders to see the future — except, that is, for those who are blessed by a *zalshagri* bond."

It's a pretty slim lead, but the only thing I was sure of in that flash of feeling was that it was the future. And... the word '*zalshagri*' calls to me. I have no idea what it means, only that it feels familiar, like the name of a long-ago ancestor.

I turn all of this over in my mind, as I wing my way to my destination. The oddly silvery and still waters of Moon's Brother Lake shine beneath me soon enough. Half-furling my wings, I take a long slow descent to the doors of the Reider Monastery.

"Good afternoon, King Avirix," comes a mellow voice, as my feet touch the ground. "We the Reiders are honored by your visit. I have been waiting for you."

"What?" I gawk at the priest. "You're — waiting for me?"

How on earth did this guy know I was coming? I didn't tell a single person about this trip.

"My morning meditation with our oldest Soul Tree showed you to me," explains the priest with a gentle smile.

"My communing with the Tree's sacred energies told me quite clearly that you would seek knowledge here today."

This guy knew I was coming because... a tree told him?

All Drokan revere trees. It is told that Krodo the Shaper made trees to carry our memories — but certainly none of them *talk* to us.

I want to laugh, but the amusement dies in my throat as I regard this strange priest. He seems so serious about what he's saying, and yet there's a lightness to him too. I can't quite put my finger on it, but he feels special.

"Yes," I say, trying to regain some sense of myself. "I'm here with a few questions about some old traditions I read about."

"Then you are a unique King," replies the priest softly. "We have not welcomed a member of the royal house for nearly a century. Now, why don't we continue this conversation somewhere more comfortable than the doorstep?"

The priest — whose name is Ziw — leads me through a bright and airy compound, filled with greenery. There are plants everywhere I care to look, sitting in bowls of soil on windowsills, or twining down around columns.

More astonishing, I see humans in the same garb as Ziw. They move as smoothly through the monastery as any of the Drokans.

"I had no idea there were human Reiders," I murmur to my guide.

"Ah, yes. Anyone who can quiet their minds to read the stars and sense the Soul Trees is welcome in our ranks," says Ziw with a faint smile. "Although..." His expression changes to one of deep sadness. "We have never had a Skuyr join our priesthood."

I want to say something nasty about the bastards, but I

hold my tongue. Anything except kindness and serenity seems wrong to speak into this place.

"Here we are." Ziw indicates the mossy cushioned ground in the center of a stand of young trees. "This is the Grove of Youth, where saplings will choose whether or not to become Soul Trees. An apt place for a new learner, I think."

I open my mouth to protest that I am no youth, but I am too calm to let the words fly. Instead, I sink into the soft moss at Ziw's side.

"Now. What is it you seek to know, my King?" Ziw regards me steadily, his worn hands folded in his lap.

"Well, I came across a word I didn't know while reading about myths and legends of the Drokan people," I begin. There's no way I'm mentioning Evalie or the incident that prompted my curiosity. This has to stay an impersonal inquiry, no matter how comfortable I feel here. "The word was *zalshagri*."

Saying it out loud, I feel a ripple pass through me. It's like it swelled up from the moss and then up my entire body.

"Ah, *zalshagri*." Ziw smiles. "A very important part of Drokan life, once upon a time. It means 'fated mate,' and yet it means more than that."

"More than that?"

"The *zalshagri* bond is a divine connection," explains the priest. "A blessing from the energy that suffuses all living things on this planet. A blessing seeded by Krodo the Shaper, long ago."

"Krodo?" I can't stop myself from raising my eyebrows.

"You're surprised we too worship Krodo," observes Ziw, correctly. "Of course we do. He shaped the flow of life down to the smallest seed. Through Krodo, everything is connected. A *zalshagri* pair is simply the most deeply connected any two beings can be."

"What... does that mean for the pair, then?"

"The mated couple is united in heart and soul. They can feel each other's feelings, know each other's location if apart, and sometimes even see the future that they share."

I sit, frozen by this explanation. I know I should think this is stupid. A mind reading couple? That's a bit much.

Except — it isn't. As I sit there under the young trees with Ziw, I realize that somehow... I recognize the idea.

Zalshagri.

NINETEEN

EVALIE

The last sips of tea that was supposed to help me sleep is long cold, but I'm still up and no closer to drifting off than I was a few hours ago when I first slipped into the covers.

Instead, I pace in front of the window.

Mar's warning about not falling for a Drokan is running through my mind. I had tried to dismiss it as over-worrying on her part. Or a misreading of signals regarding how I feel for Avirix.

But I know the feeling that's growing in my heart. And I know that Mar's warning carries some validity.

To top it all off, there's Rrame's constant badgering of my mom. That's bound to escalate if I don't head it off.

And I thought coming to the palace was going to solve some of our problems...

Finally, I throw a shawl on over my night clothes and step out into the palace halls. I wander without much thought on where I might be heading. I just need to expel this energy.

I turn a corner and bump into two palace guards on

patrol. There's been more and more of them wandering the palace at all hours of the day and night ever since the attack.

They give me a quizzical look and I quickly try to come up with some excuse for why I'm wandering around in the middle of the night.

"Um. Where's the library?" It's the first thing that pops into my mind.

The guards exchange doubtful glances with each other. Still, my position as nanny to two royal children gives me some status. Enough for them not to scoff in my face and demand I tell them what I'm really up to.

A few moments later, I'm standing stupidly in the entry way to the library. Well, maybe a boring book on Drokan history will be the soporific I need?

Going in, I'm surprised to see some candles are lit. I guess royalty can afford to keep empty rooms lighted. It'd be sacrilege back in Besiel.

Except, as it turns out, the library is *not* empty.

"My Lord," I exclaim as I step into the row between shelves of books and discover Avirix standing there.

He quickly slams closed the book in his hand and holds it behind himself.

I suddenly become aware of the slight chill in the library and pull my shawl over myself and around my arms.

"Evalie..." he says, finally. "What are you doing up?"

"I couldn't sleep," I confess.

"Really? I spend ten minutes with the twins and I feel like I could sleep for days... Perhaps a... drink would help?"

"Sure. Just point me toward the official palace bar."

"The palace doesn't have an official bar, as such."

"No, I know, I was –"

"The library liquor trolley, however," he goes on,

turning to point at a corner of the library, "is right over there."

He leads me over there. As we go, I try to scan the books on the shelves he was standing before. They look like ancient tomes of Drokanian myths or something.

When I join Avirix at the little trolley full of bottles in the library's corner, the book he had is nowhere in sight. He's already poured me a glass of something golden and smokey. I take a sip. It burns my throat just a little going down, then immediately gives me a pleasant feeling in my head.

The running thoughts start to jog lightly. A few more sips and they'll be hitting the showers, I think.

"What book were you reading?" I dare to ask. Avirix clearly isn't ignorant, but nothing about him has struck me as someone who would do research in the middle of the night.

"I wasn't actually reading it," he says quickly. "I was... I'd only just... begun... *perusing* it."

"Ah. I see." Weird response. But he *is* royalty. And royalty is sometimes pretty weird. "On a subject that was keeping you up at night?" I dare to press.

"I suppose so. Falling easily to sleep is a luxury few Kings enjoy."

"Heavy is the head the crown sits on."

"Yes. Very true. Like nannies, I suppose."

I smile and realize I've already drunk most of the liquor. I offer my glass toward him. He drains his and pours me more.

"I was researching some of our more obscure myths. Trying to answer a question."

I settle onto the edge of a deep leather chair and look up at him.

"I don't know many Drokan myths," I tell him. "But I would love to hear."

"Oh." He considers that. "What do you know of Krodo the Shaper?"

"That he shaped things?"

Avirix smiles, then settles into a chair across from me.

"Krodo the Shaper was a Drokan who lived long ago. Before we knew ourselves as we do now. The Shaper was imbued with the life force energy, which was gifted to him by the divine beings who hailed from the stars.

"Krodo's first act of love for our world was to shape the eldest trees. Into their sap, he imbued memory, so that these trees hold our most ancient secrets for all times. Their fruits taste of nostalgia. To eat one is to chew on a memory you cannot quite place, for it is the memory of the planet itself.

"When we die, we shall become the earth that helps feed the trees of memory. We shall be memory, too. And the trees shall then remember all that made up our lives. So no one is ever truly forgotten. And no Drokan life is meaningless."

His low, rumbling voice, and the poetry of the story, have lulled me. I'm leaning forward on the edge of the chair, toward him.

"Only Drokan lives are not meaningless?" I ask softly, my eyes locked on his.

"So the myths state. But I choose to believe that it applies to *all* life."

"That's good to know."

We are quiet, barely whispering. Our faces are close. I could sit forward a little more and kiss him.

But he breaks the eye contact. He looks at the floor, though I notice that his eyes linger somewhere else, first. I realize that, in leaning forward, my night shirt has drooped low, offering him an unimpeded view most of the way down my shirt, and at my bare breasts.

I should move. Sit back. Pull the shawl tighter around me.

I don't do either of those things.

TWENTY

AVIRIX

Of all the damn things...

How is it possible that she interrupted me while I was looking through a book on fated mates?!

I'd specifically come to the library *in the middle of the night* so as not to attract any attention to the research I was doing. Then Evalie, of all people, comes strolling in!

What the hell is she doing up, anyway? And what made her want to come to the library, for the love of Krodo?

And what the hell was I doing staring down her shirt? I've really lost it.

I just hope I've covered enough that she's not going to dig any further into what I was reading. She definitely seemed captivated by the myth I just shared with her about Krodo and the trees...

"So, *you* choose to believe the myth refers to all life," I hear her say as I stare at my slippered feet, "but do the myths actually talk at *all* about humans? Or strictly Drokan?"

I'm relieved that she's still discussing myth. Maybe she

didn't notice the glance I stole at the gorgeous mound of her breasts disappearing into the dark of her shirt. Maybe she didn't notice the section of the library we were in...

"Well, the myths themselves are unclear," I say, glad for the distraction. I look up and meet her gaze. She's still leaning toward me, her shirt still falling open slightly. But I focus on answering her question. "They imply a mostly Drokan slant. However, there are collections of myths that are less specific, where it is possible that the stories also speak of humans. Or, possibly are speaking *only* about humans."

"That's promising."

"For the most part, though, it's true, in the myths, the Drokan have primacy."

"Not just in myth," Evalie mutters.

There it is again, I note with disappointment. Her sense that Drokan live lives of privilege at the expense of humans. Certainly, my predecessors had ideas of Drokan supremacy over all the others on the planet – humans and Skuyr. But my governing principles have been vastly different.

"You know," I say, eager for her approval, "my reign has seen a great number of reforms to how humans are treated in the Plains."

She perks up at that. I go through a list of healthcare policies I've enacted, trade negotiations we've enacted, farming allowances, and more.

"Those are all wonderful," she says. I feel a flash of pride. "However," she goes on, and I feel the pride quickly ebb out of me, "they aren't enough."

"Change happens incrementally," I say. As soon as the words leave my mouth, I realize they're not mine. They're the words of Grall and my other advisors.

"Maybe the kind of change you're enacting is incremental. But the suffering in Besiel increases *exponentially*. While we wait for the change to catch up to our needs, people are sick, broke, dying, or worse."

"What is worse than death?" I ask, certain she's becoming hyperbolic.

"Despair is worse than death," she tells me, her voice flat and serious.

I fall quiet. She seems to think my silence is an invitation to speak more.

"Look at the Skuyr," she starts. I look up sharply. "Look, I believe violence is *never* OK. And to say I was terrified during the attack, before you saved me, would be an understatement."

"But," I insert for her.

She hesitates, then decides to tell me the truth. I don't know that I want to hear it. But I am definitely enamored of her tenacity.

"But," she says, "from what I know about the Pilger rebellion... it's possible the Skuyr have a point."

"What?"

"Maybe you need to consider reforming the way workers are treated, too."

I have about a dozen retorts ready to throw at her, but I clamp my mouth on them. I grab my glass and stare into it. My ice cube has melted, turning the golden liquor a sort of dark orange.

I consider smashing the glass on the floor. Walking away. Letting servants clean up the mess.

Which makes me think of my niece and nephew, on their knees alongside the servants and helping clean up after the food fight. I remember watching them as they put into practice the lessons Evalie has taught them about dealing with the consequences of their actions.

In some ways, Evalie isn't wrong about the Pilger rebellion. Their conditions are less than ideal. However, the situation that has spurred their rebellion is not my fault. The decisions that led to that were made by my father long before I took over the throne.

I am trying to deal with the consequences of those decisions. Perhaps, though, I need to do a better job taking responsibility for the actions of my family.

Once again, I meet her gaze. To her credit, despite her criticisms of a royal, she has not backed away. There is no apology in her eyes. I wonder if she knows that not a single other person in this palace, human *or* Drokan, would ever dare to say half as much as she's just said to me. Not even Grall on his most disagreeable day would criticize me so directly.

I should be offended. I should scoff at her peasant's concerns.

I'm not. I don't.

Instead, I'm attracted by her thoughtfulness, her convictions, and her idealism. What could I do with a woman like her beside me on the throne, advising me, guiding me...

Caring for me?

I long to kiss her. To pull her night shirt down and uncover the little bit of her that it continues to hide from me. It would be so easy to begin. I barely have to lean forward and our lips would be touching. She may have problems with my rule, but something in the air between us tells me she would have no protest to me initiating contact.

"Let me escort you back to the nursery," I hear myself saying.

Abruptly, I stand. Then she stands. I can feel her confusion, even though she says nothing.

We walk back to the nursery more or less in silence. It

occurs to me again to wonder why she's up this late. She went to visit her mother earlier in the day, I remember. I wonder if something happened...

I consider asking, but stop myself. If she wanted to share details of her family life, she would do so. Instead, I point out a few of the art work and pottery along our route back to the nursery, providing some details about the historic nature of the work or highlights of the artist.

Then we say a quiet goodnight. She thanks me for the drink and the myths. Then the nursery door closes with her on the other side.

I hurry back to the library to get the book on fated mates before returning to my own room.

TWENTY-ONE

EVALIE

"Stay off the flowers, please," I remind Or for the twelfth time in as many minutes.

I've brought the twins out to the garden to play post-lunch. It was a decision born partly out of wanting to give them fresh air and partly out of my needing to get over the fear that struck me every time I considered coming here.

Any evidence of the Skuyr attack on us here has been removed. Trampled plants have been replaced. Blood has been washed away. It's as beautiful and pictorial as it was in the moments leading up to the assault on us.

In some ways, that's healing. In others, it's eerie. As if the thing my brain knows happened never really happened.

I'm lost in these thoughts when I hear squeals of delight from the kids that bring me out of myself.

"Uncle Avirix!"

I instinctively rise from the stone bench I'm on. Avirix kneels to greet the twins and they're immediately on him. Tali hugs him. Or is doing something that is either a hug or an attempt to tackle the King of the Plains.

Even as he greets them, I see Avirix shoot a look over their heads to me. I think he's pleased to see me. He smiles. I return the smile. The whole thing is downright domestic. Familial.

Dammit, I am royally fucked. Well. Not 'royally fucked', technically. Not yet. I mean... Aw, shit. I really like this guy.

"C'mere," Avirix says to the kids as he sets himself on the bench opposite from where I am. He nods with his head for me to sit as well. Then he pats the bench on either side of him and the kids join him. "I thought I would tell you about your father," he says.

The kids fall silent, expectant.

"Now, let me see," Avirix begins. "Did you know your daddy was a troublemaker?"

"Like me?" asks Or.

"Yes," Avirix says with a laugh. "A little bit like you. For example, do you see the bench your nanny is sitting on?" Three sets of eyes land on me. I shift on the seat. "That used to be a *guffala* plant. A very rare import from the Mountain Drokan. A gift given to my great-grandfather."

"And they turned it into a *bench*?" asks Tali.

"Not exactly. They had to put the bench there after your father destroyed that tree."

"Whaaa?" two tiny voices ask in a mix of awe and wonder.

Avirix goes on to tell a story of Iziqon's misadventures as a young boy that led to him trying to use the rubbery plant as part of a catapult to launch himself over the garden wall. The end result was a broken arm for the young prince and a snapped *guffala* plant.

The twins are rapt. Avirix immediately launches into a series of tales. One involving him and his brother and an elaborate prank they pulled on an official from the Desert Drokan that nearly resulted in a war. Another about the time Iziqon was learning to pilot a convey and his antics forced the trainer – who had decades of experience – to resign.

Then he switches gears, becoming more serious if not quite somber. He relates a tale about a difficult time in his own life, and the wisdom his brother imparted to him.

"It was when my father was first becoming ill, and I realized that my time as King was coming soon. I was terrified."

"You were?" Tali asks in disbelief.

"Of course. It's a lot of responsibility to be the King. And you can't show anyone that you're nervous, or they'll wonder if you really *should* be King. But your father could tell I was in distress. One evening, we were sharing tea right here, in the garden. We'd been talking about inconsequential things. The winner of the latest Qui-pon games or something."

"I love Qui-pon," Or whispers.

"Like your daddy," Avirix offers as an aside. Then he continues, "Anyway, we'd fallen silent. And out of nowhere, your brother says, 'As King, you'll have advisors and you may even trust a few of them. But at the end of the day, it will be your decision.' Then he looked at me..."

Avirix pauses. I can he's choked up and I realize these stories are as much about his own healing as they are about informing the kids.

"He looked at me," Avirix continues, "and says, 'The most important advisor you have is yourself, Avirix. And you have good instincts. More. You have a good heart.'" He takes a deep breath. "I try every day as King to prove that your father was right about me."

A silence falls over the garden. Even the birds seem to pause in their singing. Then, Tali speaks up.

"Uncle Avirix? Why did the bad men come here the other night?"

The question pulls Avirix out of his reverie. It seems to stump him for a moment. I consider telling Tali that now is not the time for a question like that. Something makes me swallow the chastisement, though.

"It's a good question, Talissa," Avirix says slowly. "The truth is... The truth is that they were people who were very unhappy with the way the world works. And they thought they had a good solution."

"But they were hurting people."

"Yes. I guess they thought they were justified, because they feel as if they have been hurt, too."

"Well... if the world isn't working," Or says innocently, "then why don't you just fix it. You're the King!"

Avirix stares at the boy. Then at me. He cocks an eyebrow.

Oh fuck, I think. I can feel myself blush.

"It's clear who raised these children," the King says. His face is dour. Then, a half-smile appears. "Someone who is a very passionate and charming idealist."

His gaze lingers on me.

Is he flirting with me?

"And she did a good job of it, too," he says, breaking eye contact with me and smiling at the kids. Yet I can feel the way his focus is still with me.

Hey, King, I want to say to him, *this is not helping me with the feels I've got for you. Maybe back off with the compliments and sexy half-smiles, OK?*

Obviously, I don't say that, either. Thankfully, the kids have had enough of stories and political talk. They drag

Avirix off the bench and coax him into playing their games. Which mostly involves him chasing them all over the place.

"Stay off the flowers, please," I remind the King of the Plains.

TWENTY-TWO

AVIRIX

The sun is setting, but my day isn't done.

I need to see the Reiders again. I need to speak to Ziw. I need to ask how someone would know if he'd found his *zalshagri*.

I'm sure the priest will guess this question is of a more personal nature, but perhaps he already knows. If I really was the first royal to visit the monastery in a century, and my question just happened to be about the *zalshagri* bond... it doesn't take a wise man to figure it out.

And Ziw seems to be a very, very wise man.

The trip seems shorter this time, or perhaps it's simply that I'm certain of the way. Or perhaps it's that when Moon Brother's Lake spreads out beneath me, I feel almost lost in the stars twinkling in its mirror-like waters. No wonder my people believe divine beings came from the heavens.

I never gave that belief much thought, I just accepted it. I suppose if pressed I would have said it was a meaningful metaphor at this point, no matter what the historical truth of the matter may be.

Now, I'm beginning to believe that the stars genuinely

were the source of something holy. If I'm even entertaining the idea that Evalie and I have some mystical bond then... there are more marvels in the world than I ever imagined.

When I land, Ziw is again waiting for me, despite the darkness. He smiles at me, and hefts a tankard.

"Good to see you again, King Avirix." He bows, ever so slightly. "Tonight, perhaps we might chat by the lakeside? I've brought something that will keep us warm."

"Thank you, Ziw." I follow the priest as he unerringly picks his way across the shadowy ground. "I appreciate you receiving me at such a late hour."

"It is not so late," observes Ziw. "We must stay up long enough to spend some time with the stars, after all."

"They are very beautiful tonight," I say, the wonder from my flight drifting into my voice.

"Yes, and communicative." Ziw takes a seat on a long bench, carved into the side of a massive boulder at the lake's edge. "They say change is coming. Nothing more specific than that, at least not tonight, but on some kind of change they insist."

"I see."

I don't, really, but now isn't the moment for me to ask for a lesson on reading the stars. Instead, I take the tankard Ziw offers me and take a long sip, expecting tea or something.

It is not tea.

"By Krodo," I cough out, through the burn of alcohol on the back of my throat. "You monk-types DRINK?"

"Of course we do," replies Ziw serenely. He takes a sip bigger than mine, enough to make my eyes water merely contemplating it. "Fermentation is a part of the natural cycle. If left alone, fruit creates alcohol. It is a stage of the world's life, so we must not eschew it."

"That's the fanciest justification for a drink I've ever heard," I mutter before I can stop myself.

Ziw surprises me by bursting out laughing. His deep laugh echoes across the starlit waters.

"I suppose it must be," he agrees, when he's gotten a hold of himself. "Now my King, you didn't come here to discuss Reider drinking habits. What can I help you with?"

I take another swallow of liquor, this one more modest.

"How would you know if you were mated?" I ask, deciding I might as well be upfront. "How would I know if someone were my *zalshagri*?"

Amusement suffuses Ziw's face, and he grins at me. It should be a boyish expression, yet on Ziw it still looks perfectly dignified.

"I wondered when you might ask that," he says lightly. "But the answer may not be very satisfying. Meeting one's *zalshagri* can be very different depending on one's openness to the bond. The only remarkable thing that may happen is upon the *zalshagri* pair's first touch, skin to skin."

"Oh?" My heart thumps in my chest. "And what is that?"

"If one is already contemplating a connection, then they may sense a glimpse of the future. I say sense, because the impression this dizzying moment leaves is more one of feelings than events."

"I — I see," I stammer, hearing in Ziw's words something that sounds a lot like the flash I experienced. "But... how can anyone be certain? A momentary glimpse isn't enough."

"Well, the only true way to be sure is to spend time with your potential mate." Ziw tilts his head at me, eyes warm. "See if you feel different. You'd feel more content, perhaps more free and light-hearted. You might even feel physically healthier."

I nod slowly, taking this in. All of those feelings might be coincidences, though... certainly I can't separate my joyousness at being around Evalie from being around the kids right now.

"However — something you must know is that for the *zalshagri* bond to be cemented, both parties MUST accept it," cautions Ziw. "A one-sided bond will ultimately fail."

"And what is that failure?"

"The connection dies away, like an unwatered seedling." Ziw spreads his hands. "Like all living things, the *zalshagri* bond must be tended."

We converse a little more after that, but Ziw can tell he's answered my question and I'm raring to go. Soon enough he drains his entire damn tankard, and gets up to return to the monastery.

"Follow your soul, King Avirix," he says, by way of parting words. "It is the only thing that can guide you in this."

"That is easier said than done."

Ziw gives me an enigmatic smile.

"How much do you know of our ancient tales, King Avirix?" he asks me.

I shug and do my best to be neutral in my response, "I know of your sect and what the main beliefs are. Of a connected world."

"There is so much more than that, King," Ziw states. "Fated mates were once much more common than they are in our complicated world. In the time of Kincaid--"

"Time of Kincaid the Trickster?" I interrupt him. This is getting ridiculous.

"Kincaid came to us from the stars, and he was embraced by the Skuut."

"Skuut?"

"My apologies," Ziw says. "I meant the Skuyr."

"Apparently you've been drinking a lot longer than you let on," I laugh.

"Our world has many secrets, King," Ziw continues. "Have you never wondered how Skuyr, Drokan, and human came to live as they do on this planet?"

"This is the way of things," I reply. "Three races have always shared Genesis. With the Drokan as leaders."

"And how did the Drokan become the leaders?"

I pause.

"They followed their souls, those early Drokan, King Avirix," Ziw says to me. "By the Life Tree's guidance they followed their souls. As you must do now."

Those words run through my head as I fly slowly home. The cold air goes right to my head, making my very thoughts crisp.

I need some time with Evalie, just the two of us. Planned time, not an accidental library run-in. Focused time, to see if there's anything to this mate business.

As I mull this over, I stumble on an idea. I could take Evalie into the city — no prying palace eyes, and plenty to do in case things get awkward.

And what will I do about those prying palace eyes if Evalie and I are zalshagri?

I grind my teeth, as the lights of the palace come into view. Indeed, having a human queen would spark massive objections and create many issues. But...

I'll worry about that when — IF — it happens.

I land in the gardens, to gain myself a little extra walking time to my room. I'm thinking through all the things Evalie and I could do in the city, when I practically bump into Grall.

"Your majesty," comes that grating voice. "I saw you fly in. Where in Krodo's name have you been, with no escort?"

"Oh, nowhere dangerous," I reply thoughtlessly, only wanting to get rid of Grall as quickly as possible. "Only the Reider monastery."

I've said the wrong thing.

Grall draws himself upright and gives me a shocked look.

"My king, I beg to differ. That sect is *quite* dangerous. The Reiders are full of jumbled and ridiculous ideas, doddering old mystics that they are. You must not give them too much credence!"

"I'm aware of their reputation," I say, even though I want to defend Ziw and all his brethren. "I simply had a question about a myth. And, the Reiders are my people, too."

Grall opens his mouth, obviously about to argue more, but I've had enough of his narrow-mindedness.

"Good night, Grall," I tell him firmly. "We'll speak more tomorrow."

He stays quiet as I stride away. I should consider that a success but instead... it makes me oddly nervous.

TWENTY-THREE

EVALIE

The kids are down for their afternoon nap and I'm somewhere between a daydream and a doze when there's a light knock on the doors to the nursery.

Before I can answer, the door swings open and Avirix appears, along with an elderly Drokan woman.

"Ohh," the woman says in a voice that is still sprightly despite her years, "it looks just like it did..."

"Ah, Evalie," Avirix says, seeing me. "Perfect. This is Yakwa. She was my and my brother's nanny when we were young."

"Back when they called me Ya-ya," the elderly woman says with a smile. Her eyes crinkle so much they're almost lost in the folds of her wrinkles. I'm immediately in love with her. I imagine that any tenderness that lies beneath Avirix's royal demeanor must have been given to him via osmosis from Ya-ya.

"It's a pleasure to meet you," I say. "But... am I being replaced?"

"Only for the day," Avirix says with a smile. Then, seeing I don't get it, he goes on. "I thought you could use a break, Evalie. So I managed to convince Yakwa to come out retirement for a day to relieve you."

"Not that I was ever able to convince this one to take time off and play, even as a boy," Yakwa says, nudging the King with her elbow. "Only Iziqon could ever get him to stop being so serious." Then the old lady sighs. She reaches up and places a hand on Avirix's cheek. "Oh... your poor brother," she says.

Avirix nods solemnly. He takes her hand from his cheek and holds it a moment. Their familiarity is sweet. Then Avirix turns back to me.

"Of course," he says, and I detect something that sounds almost like hesitancy in his voice, "the day is yours to do with as you please. *However*... if you would like... That is, if it might be of interest to you... I would like to invite you to see the city with me."

His words paralyze me. I think I've said something, but I'm not actually able to utter words. *Is he asking me on a date?*

"Am I right in thinking," Avirix goes on, "that you've never seen much of it?"

"No. I mean, yes. You're right. In thinking. That I have. Not." *Oh boy. Yakwa must think I'm a moron.*

"Well then," Avirix says, clearing his throat, "would you allow me to give you a tour?"

"My Lord... it is a lovely offer..."

"Oh, girl, he's not just being polite," Yakwa says. I look at her and there's a twinkle in her eye that seems to align with my instincts about what's going on.

"Ya-ya, please," Avirix mutters to her, a little boy again.

I think of Mar's advice. That I should stay away from him. That nothing good can come of following my feelings for him.

"Yes, My Lord," I say, "I would very much enjoy that."

The next thing I know, I'm traveling inside a Lev, taking a lovely hovercraft along one of the elevated tubes that traverses the city. The view of the most luxurious places in Besiel is pretty stunning. I almost forget that this Drokan wealth and commerce sits atop the slums I and my race are from.

We're taking crystal-powered public transit. Avirix has disguised himself for the affair. He's got a long robe with a hood, plain pants and tunic and worn boots. However, his 'plebian' wardrobe is out of date. The fashions he's sporting are about ten years old.

"You look like some Drokan grandpa," I mutter, taking my eyes from the city a moment.

"I do not," he says, his voice betraying the fact that he knows damn well he does.

"We didn't have to do public transportation."

"You can *see* the city from the sky," he tells me, "but you *experience* it on the ground. Don't worry. I've done this before."

"When? A decade ago?" I ask, again in reference to his clothes.

"No. It was..." I watch him do the math in his head, then fall silent. I was right.

Then, a stop is announced and the tube's doors swing open. Avirix takes my hand and we hop off the Lev. He doesn't tell me where we're going and I don't care. The sights all along the way are enough to occupy me. Merchants hawking wares I've never seen. Male and female Drokan in fashions that make my jaw drop. Beautiful architecture. Crystal-powered tech all over the place.

"Here, this is it. My great-grandfather had this installed..."

I turn my attention to where Avirix has brought me. We are in the middle of a mall, surrounded by low-rise buildings that all appear to have some sort of government function. In the middle of the mall, there is a reflecting pool. Hovering just above the water, powered by mini-crystals, float little lights that move in varying speeds about the pool.

At first, I think their movements are random. Then, I detect patterns. Then, I realize what I'm seeing. The lights, pairing with the reflections in the pool, are creating symmetrical images. Some of the images are pretty and abstract. Others represent outlines of a Drokan. Or of a Plains-specific bird or flower.

"How beautiful," I say.

We're both leaning on the rail that runs the perimeter of the pool. I notice that our arms are brushing one another. Neither of us moves to create more space.

"As the stars come out," Avirix explains softly, his voice a kind of romantic burr, "the lights take on the patterns in the sky. They move as the constellations move through the sky, over the course of the year."

"It's very lovely."

There are speakers all along the pool that play very soft music, mostly Drokan pipes and string instruments. I don't know much about Drokan songs, but I believe it's an instrumental version of an old love ballad. I ask Avirix if I'm right.

He listens a moment, surprised.

"Yes. You're exactly right," he says. He listens another moment, then looks down at me.

We share a gaze like the umpteen other gazes we've shared since we first met. The gaze that usually ends with one of us awkwardly breaking out of it. This time, neither one of us looks away. There is just us, the music, and the dancing lights in the reflecting pool.

I have so much I want to say to him. But I also have this weird sensation. Like he already knows the words I would speak. Like they are the words on the tip of his tongue, too.

Don't be such a romantic, I scold myself. *It's not like there's some invisible force bonding the two of you.*

It's a lovely moment, nevertheless.

TWENTY-FOUR

AVIRIX

I can't believe I never before noticed that music playing by the reflecting pool. I guess subconsciously I knew it was there. But until Evalie focused my attention on it, I hadn't realized the specific song.

But this is what it's like with her. She makes me see things in the world in ways I've never seen before. Even the reflecting pool and the lights. I've been familiar with them for my entire life. Yet now, this afternoon, it's as though I'm seeing them anew. Because I am, in part, seeing them through her eyes.

Is that a confirmation of the *zalshagri* bond?

Or is the fact that every time we touch, even the barest amount, even briefly, my body hums?

As we stood staring into the pool, our arms were just brushing against each other. The intensity of emotion I was feeling was nearly too much to handle. Like whatever the *good* version of pushing on a bruise is.

We move away from the pool and I show her around the mall. A few glances come our way, but from their sniggers, it seems that their looks are directed more at my outfit than the fact that I'm their King in disguise.

Someone mutters something about looking like I jumped out of a time machine as she walks by.

"What did that woman say?" Evalie asks with a smirk, knowing full well what she said.

"I didn't hear anything," I say hastily. "Let me show you this here..."

Eventually, we're both getting hungry. Luckily, the mall is near Mavara's. It's one of the fanciest restaurants in my kingdom. Also one of the most delicious. Owned by a chef couple named Uigor and Klostafer (the restaurant's name is also their daughter's), I'd been coming there since I was young. Uigi and Klos – as they insist on being called – now treat me almost like any other customer that visits them.

So the staff barely bat an eyelash as I step to the restaurant's hostess and remove my cloak. In the whole place, there's only one busser who seems unable to keep his eyes off me. That's the sort of tact that keep people like me – and the rest of the Plains Kingdom's well-to-do – comfortable and regular customers.

That tact always extends to my guests. Even, I'm relieved to see, if it's a human woman. She's probably the only human in here who isn't working. And even the members of the staff who *are* human are kept in jobs that relegate them to the kitchen.

Which is something I realize I've never really been cognizant of until right this moment.

Something else to which my eyes have been opened by Evalie.

I'm pondering that when Uigi and her husband, Klos, emerge from the kitchen. I don't even know how the hostess got them word I was here, but there you have it. They coo at me and at Evalie as they welcome us.

"What do I need to have tonight, Uigi?" I ask.

"Klos will tell you the baked *rugha*," she says loudly.

"What will *you* tell me?"

"The baked *rugha* is delicious," she says noncommittally. Then, in a whisper to me, she adds, "But my pan-seared *wiykya* with *potarune* sauce is divine."

"Uigi, you know I am a sucker for anything in a *potarune...*"

"Oh, is that so, My Lord... good to know." But of course she knows. She probably knows what I like to eat better than I do.

On our way to the table, I note the busser still agog at me. That's disconcerting. I realize I don't recognize him. Must be new. Finally, a more experienced busser yanks at his horns and sends him back to work.

Uigi and Klos deposit us in our seats. There is a whirl of activity as servers surround us, putting napkins in our lap, filling our water glasses, dropping hearth-baked bread on the table.

Evalie takes it all in with the same wonder as she did the reflecting pool. I wonder if I've overshot a little? Will she be intimidated? Will this display of wealth turn her off?

I'm suddenly having second thoughts.

"Is this... all right?" I ask.

"If the food is half as good as the service and the décor, I think I'm in for the meal of my life."

I sigh inwardly.

"Let me tell you this," I say, "the service and the décor are *three-fourths* as good as the food."

The wine-steward, an elderly Drokan with drooping

wings but an elegant air, appears beside our table with a bottle.

"Ah, Offis," I say, pleased to see him. "I'm glad to see you're back."

"Just a little cold, my Lord. I was barely out a day. Just happened to be the one during which you stopped by. I hope things didn't turn out too poorly."

"On the contrary, the steward you're training gave you a run for your money. What have we tonight?"

Offis presents the bottle. A hundred-and-fifty-year-old Plains varietal. I play along as he goes through the motion of letting me taste, as if there was any chance that I wouldn't like it.

Then Offis is gone and Uigi and Klos come by to see if we want to order anything specific or trust them.

"Whatever you recommend, Klos," I say, with a wink past him to his wife. Then they, too, depart.

Evalie stares at me slack-jawed.

"What?" I ask.

"Nothing. 'Hi, Offis.' 'Oh, good to see you Uigi.' 'Hey there, Klos.' 'What's up, Huey, Duey and Louie?'"

"All right," I say good-naturedly, waving off the joke. "What can I say? I try to make a little effort to get to know my people directly. Shouldn't a King do just that?"

"I think a King definitely should," she says with a warm smile. Then, I see something shift in her eyes. And I can sense what's coming. The idealist in her is about to speak. "But have you ever made an effort to get to know the Skuyr directly? Or any humans?"

I was hoping we could have an evening free of political conversation. I lean forward over the table toward her and smile.

"I'm making quite an effort right now to get to know a human," I say.

It has my intended effect on her. She blushes, smiles a smile that I have to believe bounces light off every glass and dish and piece of silverware in the room.

Then the first course is upon us and our meal is full of laughter, fine wine and deliciousness. Our talk flows effortlessly. A mix of laughter, revelation, personal insight, and mutual appreciation.

It's as though we were made to spend this sort of time together.

Or fated to.

TWENTY-FIVE
EVALIE

As we sit in Mavara's, mostly I'm just enjoying myself. For long spans of time, I'm able to let the flow of easy conversation, delicious wine, and incredible food take over my senses. Yet here and there, the inner monologue sneaks in.

This is a date. This is a DATE. Right?

No. No way is this a date. The King of Plains would not date a human. FUCK a human, maybe.

I feel like all of a sudden I have two personalities living in my head: the one certain that Avirix is courting me, and the one who screams a version of my mother's warning at me at every opportunity.

As Avirix consults with the owner on a round of desserts, I try to settle my brain. I don't know anything for sure, other than that Avirix is showing me a lot of personal attention.

Besides, whatever Avirix's motives are, I can't believe they're solely carnal. This is A LOT of effort to put in just to have sex. He's the gorgeous King of the Plains, too — I bet he could have anyone he wanted.

And... I can't deny that Avirix shows me a lot of tenderness. I may be letting my desire for him make me foolish, but I know tender when I feel it. Plus... it might be stupid, but... I trust him.

I straighten as Avirix turns back to me with that devastating smile on his face. He's obviously excited about dessert, which is adorably boyish for a King.

Okay. No more obsessing over it — I'm having a great time and that is that.

"How many desserts did you just order?" I ask, with an amused smile. "Three? Five? Eighteen? Two hundred and seven?"

"Oh, not that many." Avirix claps his hand to his heart. "Only forty-one, please. I am a Drokan of great restraint."

We burst into giggles, more than the silly joke deserves. I think the wine is going to our heads. Or at least, it's going to mine and Avirix is content to follow my lead.

Like the wine steward is determined to see us both tipsy, a new wine arrives. The fellow (Offis, I believe?) explains that it is perfectly balanced to complement the sweets.

Well in that case, how can I say no?

Avirix and I are ooh-ing and aah-ing about the delectable floral notes in this new vintage, when I begin to hear something odd.

"Is someone shouting outside?" I cock my head, listening harder to the world beyond the serene restaurant. "Are several someones shouting outside?"

Avirix pauses in the middle of lifting his wine glass to his lips.

"Yes," he says thoughtfully. "And they're getting louder."

Uigi comes out from the back, carrying two plates of

dessert. She frowns as she too takes in the noise outside Mavara's. Sweeping to our table, she sets down the sumptuous confections.

"One moment, my Lord," she murmurs. "Let me go see what that commotion is about."

Avirix and I both watch Uigi as she moves to the door. She opens it, and a flood of yells suddenly fill the space.

"King Avirix! King Avirix! Come out!"

"My King! Please, I must speak to you!"

"Let us inside, we know the King is in there!"

Abruptly, Uigi slams the door shut. It shudders as someone thuds into it, but Uigi doesn't seem phased. She shoots a large bolt home with a look of deep irritation on her features.

"Who was it?" she demands of the restaurant. "Which one of you dared to breach MY hospitality by spreading word of King Avirix's presence?"

The other wealthy Drokan eating all look shocked. I'm not sure if it's at the idea that they would be so gauche as to rat out Avirix, or at the tone with which this older female is speaking to them. Either way, the looks on their faces make me want to giggle.

"Uigi!" calls Avirix, his eyes raking across the room. "I don't think it was a customer. I think it was your new busboy. I noticed him staring at me earlier and now he's gone."

Uigi curses creatively (which also makes me want to giggle) and yells for her husband. Then she turns to our table and sighs.

"Well, you best be out the back. The sooner those idiots out front see you're nowhere in here, the sooner things can go back to peace and quiet."

Like she summoned it, there's a banging on the door.

"So sorry, my lord," her husband says as he rushes out of the kitchen. "Right this way."

Avirix looks at Klos, looks at me, looks at the two desserts on the table. He stands up, but not before grabbing a napkin and shoving the purple cake dessert into it.

That does it.

The King of the Plains Drokan, refusing to leave his dessert behind?

All the giggles I've held back begin to escape my mouth as the two of us rush to the back of the restaurant. My laughter infects Avirix, and he begins to chuckle too. We're like two school kids sneaking out of class, PLUS Avirix has cake clutched in his fist.

We're still giggling as we push through the door out into the night — and find even more people waiting for us.

"King Avirix!" shouts one, reaching out to grab the sleeve of Avirix's terrible disguise. "You must hear my plea, my neighbor STOLE my *demsin* tree and—"

"My King, there are no doctors within easy Lev access of me and—"

"Please, please!" In vain, Avirix holds up his hand. "I hold a public audience every Firstday! Bring your queries to me then!"

But it's hopeless. There's too many of them. We try to push through, but the crowd is thickening as the ones in front hear the hubbub.

"Evalie," whispers Avirix. "Run. When I take off, run wherever you can. I promise, I'll find you."

I turn wide eyes to him, but he's already moving. Bunching his powerful legs, he launches himself high into the air. The motion causes the crowd to stagger back. I'm not so tipsy I can't see my moment.

I launch myself into motion. Contorting my narrow

frame, I slip through the gaps between people. A few male Drokans from the crowd also jump into the air, making it even easier to burst through.

I run like crazy, sparing a moment to be grateful for all the time I've spent running after Or and Tali. I'm faster than I thought I'd be, sprinting around corners and changing direction at random.

Looking up, I see Avirix's impressive wings above me. He's flying low, dodging around the same corners I am with incredible deftness. The males chasing him can't manage nearly the same moves, and drift high into the air.

Luckily for us, the shadows in the streets keep us hidden from their greedy eyes.

Finally, I can't hear anyone behind us. I come to a stop in an alleyway, panting and still half-laughing. The whole thing is so ridiculous, I can barely comprehend it.

With a gust of air, Avirix lands right next to me. One of his sapphire-veined golden wings caresses my shoulder as he folds them in. I catch my breath at the touch, and again as he turns his chiseled face to me. Sparkling merriment dances in his blue-grey eyes.

My heart thumps into a gallop at his nearness. All of a sudden, my inner monologue rears up once more, but in a single, very clear voice this time.

You know what would help you decide if this is a date? Seeing what he does if you kiss him.

So... I do.

TWENTY-SIX

AVIRIX

My body is nothing but harmony. My bones hum, low and deep, as my heart beats in perfect time and my skin positively sings.

This kiss... it's like nothing I've ever felt before. Evalie's lips are sweeter than the cake I took from Mavara's. They're richer than any wine Offis has ever given me. She tastes like everything I've ever wanted and more.

Then she pulls away, and I'm left staring at her in shock. I can't believe she kissed me. Moreover, I've never experienced anything like this — definitely not from only a simple kiss. The harmony is gone with the warmth of Evalie's mouth, but my muscles are still practically vibrating.

All I want is more.

I realize Evalie's eyes are searching my face, an uncertain smile frozen on her lips. She looks hesitant, or perhaps embarrassed. The beginning of a flush is creeping onto her delicate cheekbones.

Does she not know what she does to me?

I begin to reach for her, to show her without a shadow of

a doubt how much I want her. But before I can touch her the way my aching body demands, I hear a familiar sound.

Shouting.

"Here, he's here!" comes a cry from above.

I snap my head up, suddenly registering both the lanky Drokan youth hovering above us and the noise of a crowd. I turn around, protectively getting in front of Evalie. As soon as I do, people begin pouring into the alleyway.

Not as many as outside the restaurant to be sure, but enough.

"My *demsin* tree!" howls one.

"An invitation for my daughter—"

"A job for my brother—"

"A Lev tube out to Aemup Street—"

We're trapped. The people are pushing and shoving at each other, yelping their demands and their questions. They near us, almost so close I can feel their breath on my face.

"Avirix," whispers Evalie behind me. My heart breaks at the hint of fear in her voice. "I don't know if I can run that much more."

I glare at the oncoming mob, striving to put every ounce of displeasure I've ever felt into a very Kingly expression.

"Stand BACK!" I yell, loud enough that it startles a few into stopping. "Is this how you treat your King?"

That pauses the surging herd of people for a moment, but not for long. I have to do something. This time, I can't risk separating from Evalie. At least a few of these yipping mongrels will have noticed I'm protective of her. They might follow her.

The only way out is the sky. But how can I possibly carry Evalie much farther than a few rooftops over? She doesn't weigh much, but I've never flown a distance carrying anyone.

Yet even as I question my own ability, an unusual strength surges through me. I feel powerful, unstoppable, like there is no force in the world greater than me.

I can carry Evalie. In a flash, I just know it. I can take off with her in my arms, I can hold her as I fly, and I can make it to the palace.

"Hold on," I say, turning to her and sweeping her into my arms. I cradle her, one arm supporting her legs and the other tucked around her back. Her hands instinctively go up and around my neck, and I have to bite back a groan. How sweet, how *right* she feels, pressed against my chest.

Now is not the time for such thoughts.

From standing, without a single step and certainly without a run to help me launch myself into the air, I leap. I leap, and I'm flying, my wings beating the air down onto the people below.

There are shrieks and shouts, but they dwindle swiftly. More males get themselves airborne, but it is a trifle to leave them behind. I can hear them, flapping comically hard, in a vain effort to reach us.

Soon, there is no one but me and Evalie, gliding through the darkness. The lit city spills out beneath us, my glowing palace at one end. Above, there is light too — the ethereal silvery gleam of the stars.

"This is incredible," breathes Evalie, held snug against me. "I've never seen anything so beautiful. It's like...we're in the center of a galaxy."

"It does feel like that, doesn't it?" I dip my head, catching the intoxicating smell of her. "I'm so glad to share this with you."

"Me too," murmurs Evalie, and I can feel her heart pick

up its pace. "I didn't know you could carry someone and fly at the same time."

I stop myself from saying *Neither did I*, since that might be hard to explain. Instead, I let the smooth velvet and sparkling crystal of the night silently carry us back to the palace.

We land on my balcony. I'm careful to touch down slowly, to lower Evalie so she can get her feet under her. When I'm down too, I realize she's still standing in the circle of my arms.

My heart hammers in my chest. I feel awkward, and strange.

How do I tell her what that kiss back there meant to me? Do I simply kiss her back?

Then Evalie, with her amazing magic, pulls me back into the moment.

"Hey," she asks softly. "What happened to that cake you took?"

I gaze into her eyes, and see her charming sense of mischief in them. All awkwardness between us drops away. I give her a rakish smile, a laugh bubbling up in me as I remember.

"I dropped it," I reply, my smile widening. "When I took off the first time. So, probably on someone's head."

Evalie starts to laugh, then I start to laugh. We're half-holding each other, half-giggling out the adrenaline of the night. It's all so natural.

And so is the instant that I finally kiss her back.

This kiss is nothing like the first one. Instead of becoming a gentle harmony, my body becomes a bonfire of desire. Heat rushes through every fibre of my being, and my groin tightens with need.

Evalie is right there with me. She's wrapping herself

around me, parting her lips for my tongue. One hand clings to my bicep while the other slides over my heart.

I heft her into my arms and carry her inside where no one can see us, still kissing her. Flames lick up my ribs, making me crackle with lust. It's unbelievable, how quickly she's brought me to this point.

We tumble onto a divan, Evalie in my lap. Our mouths stay fused together, but her hands are undoing the buttons of my shirt as mine run over her mesmerizing curves. When she gets my shirt open and slides her slender palm over my bare chest, I very nearly roar.

"Evalie," I gasp, pulling away from our kiss. "I — I need." I take a deep, but only slightly steadying breath. "May I make love to you?"

"Yes," she whispers. "Stars, Avirix, *yes*."

She doesn't have to say anything more than that. I breathe her in like air, peppering kisses over every inch of her. My hands slip under her clothes, exploring her luscious softness, feeling her dizzying beauty in my fingertips.

It's not enough.

I want to *know* her. I want to see her. I want to taste her. Oh, by the Shaper, I want to taste her.

I can't stop myself from acting on that want — that *need*. Flipping us so Evalie now rests on the divan, I kneel between her legs. It is the work of a second to tug down her flowing trousers and her scrap of panties.

Leaving her bared to me, in rosy, swollen splendor.

"So beautiful," I groan, running a single finger between her nether lips. She moans, low and sweet, and I feel my cock jerk in response.

Without denying myself for another minute, I dip my head between Evalie's legs, and I finally, *finally* taste her.

TWENTY-SEVEN
EVALIE

If I were to take my last breath now, I would die happy.

It's a strange thought to have but it completely makes sense. The warmth of Avirix's tongue on me, his attentions soft but insistent, create a cascade within me. I feel like I'm the center of it all, that the energy building deep below may soon explode outwards.

Arching my head back, I close my eyes and surrender to his ministrations. His strong palms cup my backside, their soft pressure making me feel safe.

I let my hands trail down to seek out his luxurious hair. My fingers twirl and dance within the locks, pulling gently as he continues to worship me down there.

That's what it feels like. The King is worshipping me.

And the cascade is growing. Like a whirlpool, it starts to take on its own energy, gathering strength as Avirix works. His tongue dances and he hums, sending delicious vibrations deep within me. I never knew such sensations could exist.

"Mmmm, yes," I breathe. The cascade is growing too big for me to contain.

You don't have to. Surrender.

Every nerve I have is alive. I reach up one hand from his hair to my breast. The nipple is hard and erect and I stroke it. It only adds to the cascade, another stream sucked into the whirlpool.

The cascade can't be stopped. Can't be contained. I can't stop it anymore. Taking in a deep breath, my body surrenders to it, utterly and completely.

"Oh! Yes!" Words escape my throat as my body is subsumed. The cascade overtakes me and I'm gone - no thoughts, no worries, no...nothing, for several seconds. It's a complete and divine release.

Seconds later, the cascade, like a sea after a storm, begins to ebb away. Small eddies cause my limbs to shudder, especially as Avirix pulls his mouth away. But I feel calm and content. The sun has returned and the waters are quiet.

Not for long, though. His body must be satiated.

True enough. Opening my eyes, I look down the length of my body and spy Avirix' face. His smile is unlike any expression I've ever seen before - boyish, unfettered, open and free. I want nothing more than to keep giving him ways to have that face. The weight of being King must be crushing.

"Thank you," I whisper.

"No, I must thank you. For that...connection. You..."

His voice trails off, his words lost. I'm not sure what he wanted to say, but we don't need words now. I just want his body near.

"C'mere..." I invite him towards me.

Still smiling his boyish smile, he peels his body away from between my legs and makes his way upwards, kissing me the entire time. Each kiss feels like a spark, igniting my skin.

As his head approaches mine, I cup both sides of his chiseled face and bring him to me, hungrily. I want his breath, his life-force, his mouth.

Our lips connect and I taste a new sweetness lingering there - me. It's dizzying and intoxicating. Perhaps that why he was rendered speechless?

Wrapping my legs around him, I kiss him deeper, stronger. Our tongues meet and entwine, as if the act of kissing could subsume us both into one being. His hands scoop under me, pulling me upwards and into him.

Our chests touch and I can feel a new cascade building, the waters of our bodies mixing and mingling, creating a mighty river.

Avirix breaks his kiss and pulls upward, his eyes locking into mine.

"Who are you? How have you come to be here?"

His searching questions feel too big to answer. I have no idea. But what I do know is that I must have him. Now.

Laughing, I kiss him once more. "I'm here. As are you. Now, let's make love."

If he was looking for permission, he got it and he smiles even more broadly at my words.

"As you wish."

Our kisses resume, a new fervor to them this time. From between my legs, I can feel his warm cock, hard and insistent, near my opening - oh so near. But, at the moment, it feels like leagues away.

My hands snake their way down to his mid-back and I let my nails lightly dance and scratch against the strong arch of his sapphire wings. It sends a shiver through him and I hear him groan in appreciation.

Breaking his kiss once more, he arches his back above me, as if preparing for something. He searches my face once more and then, with a swift surety that takes my breath away, he enters me, slow but completely on target.

It makes me gasp as the cascade ripples upon impact. His moves are slow and deliberate but the union of our bodies feels so right that I almost cry at the feeling.

A low grumble escapes him as he enters and retreats in a languid rhythm. I can tell he is trying to control himself, telling himself to savor every second, every move.

Digging my nails around the base of his wings, I pull my body upwards to him. I want the warmth generated between us never to waver, never to slacken. My breasts, rigid and alert, connect with the deep pecs of his chest - delicious and warm.

Avirix begins to thrust faster. Each thrust feels deeper and more exquisite - plumbing the depths of my being.

"Yes, oh yes," I whisper, pulling myself into him even more.

My hands slide down the base of his back and grasp his ass, hard and tight. Guiding him, I feel it move with each thrust, a powerful engine kicking the piston forward.

The thrusting intensifies. And with it, the cascade. It's building once more. And I can tell it is building within Avirix. His eyes close with pleasure and his body becomes one giant conduit, pushing and pulling against my depths.

"Now, yes, now," I breathe.

It's the permission he needed. With three last thrusts, the cascade closes over me again, this time taking Avirix with it. Our bodies shudder in unison and I hear a deep, primal groan escape the King of the Plains.

We stay like this for what seems an exquisite eternity, our bodies in perfect union. Human and Drokan, a perfect combination.

But, sadly, it cannot last. The divine is ephemeral.

Slowly, our bodies collapse in on each other. The warmth is still there, especially as Avirix' chest closes down upon my own.

His face buries in my neck. I can feel his breathing start to slow as he breathes into my neck, my ear, my hair.

"You..."

"Us."

It feels so right. We lie in warmth and joy, as sleep closes over us.

TWENTY-EIGHT

AVIRIX

I t's the shift in the light that wakes me. That and the fresh morning air - so different from the scents of the midnight hours - that forces my eyes open.

It's dawn, another day. And yet, given what happened last night, it seems as if something entirely new is being built around me, forged from my union with Evalie only hours before.

It feels so right and yet - did it really happen? Turning my head, I marvel at the sleeping form nestled within the crook of my arm, her hair an unfettered mess.

I know I shouldn't because she is still sleeping but my body curls up around her, squeezing her tight. It's like I just want to close our bodies off to the outside world, off from the encroaching morning. For with it I know will come the reality: royal duties, demands, separation.

But, for just these moments, I want us to continue floating on our own private island - just us, naked, warm and alone on my bed.

Her eyes flutter open and she smiles languidly as she gazes at me sleepily.

"Morning," she drawls, sleep still heavy on her.

"Good morning."

"It's early...you should...go back to sleep."

"I can't, not right now." It's true. My brain and body are too awake to even think of sleep. Plus, something else is on my mind...

"Oh gosh, I should get back. I've been gone too long," she says, stretching and pulling away from me.

It's too soon. Not yet.

"Just a few more minutes, please?"

"But we have imposed on Yakwa enough. I should go," she replies, though I can hear the conflict in her voice. She wants to stay too.

"Ya-Ya will understand. She always does. I am her favorite," I say, smiling, tugging at Evalie's naked body to return to me, to keep the warmth in.

"No, I must go."

"Blame me. And besides, I'm the damn king."

She stops her protests for a second and looks at me, almost as if seeing me for the first time. One of her long, beautiful hands cradles my face as her face grows serious.

"You really are, aren't you?" Her voice has a tinge of laughter and incredulity to it.

I feel exactly the same way. How did we find each other?

Moments pass and we just take each other in. Finally, she pulls away and leaves the bed, dressing quickly.

I know she must go but I hate it. Even my kingly self can't help but sulk sometimes.

Returning to the bed, she cradles my face once more.

"Thank you...for everything. I will see you soon."

Leaning over, she gives me one final kiss - deep and long, before disappearing from my room. It all happens so quickly, I have to roll over to where she lay to feel the vanishing warmth of where her body lay to make sure it was all real.

It was. It was all real. And now you know. You know it's all real.

Yes. That something else on my mind is now back, tugging at me for immediate attention. As I lie there, seeped in the afterglow of Evalie's presence, I am now certain of one thing. She is my *zalshagri* - my fated mate. It feels as right to me as the feeling of my own skin.

But what to do about it? It will surely cause some major problems at the palace.

But what did you say just now?

'And besides, I'm the damn king.'

Right. That. It is still true.

Sighing, I get out of bed. There is no hope for sleep now. May as well use these extra hours to be productive.

After washing and dressing (my thoughts inevitably drifting back to my night with Evalie), I drift to my office, prepared to tackle some long overdue matters.

The situation at Pilger demands more than a temporary solution. The issues and demands of the rebels are not going to go away. Once unleashed, they can't be unsaid. New laws must be enacted.

And, given the thoughts and passions Evalie spoke about to me, I feel inspired. Inspired that, with some negotiation and foresight, new laws could be enacted at Pilger that would bring about a new era. Perhaps of equality and, yes, dare I say it, progressive measures.

The next few hours blur by as I dive into the laws and codes that currently govern Pilger. Some edicts will have to be entirely struck, while others require only tweaking. Looking at the issues with the eyes on both sides proves useful for framing my thoughts.

It's clear that I cannot engage directly with the most violent of the rebels. But, if I concede to all their demands, local support will vanish. It's a delicate balance, but one I feel (now with Evalie's inspiration) ready to tackle.

I'm not sure what it is, but my concentration is intensely focused and I don't cease working until I hear the sound of a throat clearing somewhere above me.

Looking up, my mood instantly sours a notch or two.

Grall. Obliterating the light behind him, his ever-present staff leaning against my desk. How did he get in here without my noticing?

"Morning, Grall. I didn't hear you come in," I say, as nonchalantly as possible.

"Forgive me, Your Majesty, but it seems that we have an issue to...resolve. Concerning some rather odd behavior."

I only barely look up.

"Yes? And what is that?"

"Am I to understand that you left the palace gates last night, ventured out into public and, being spotted, caused a riot?"

How utterly Grail-like to attempt to scold a monarch,

"Perhaps. What of it?"

"In the company of a human female too? Are my scouts correct?"

Sighing, I look Grall in the eye. I will not tolerate being dressed down by an advisor.

"I was getting to know my people. What better way than to be out with them, humans included. I admit I may have been crude in my attempt, but no harm, no foul."

I hold his gaze but, to my chagrin, break it first. His beady eyes bore into me. And besides, I know that what I just said is only making my future uncertain. To deny the importance of my human female companion will not help me when I make the case for my fated mate. But I am not ready for that fight just yet. There are too many knots to be worked out. I need to make sure I know what I am doing before I engage. Especially with the likes of Grall.

"Your Majesty, the danger that brings upon you and the palace, the scandal—-"

"I have been working on new drafts for Pilger, Grall. Perhaps you would like to review?

Yes, distract the old bugger. That'll work.

Grall, like the old dog he is, ceases his meddling tone and takes the bait. Taking the proffered paper, he quickly skims my sketched outline.

My hope that he will vanish and leave me alone quickly evaporates.

"You seek...compromise? Cooperation? With rebel scum?"

"That's not how it's worded, no." I try to take the papers back from him but he deftly moves them away.

"This saddens me, Your Majesty. These measures...are weak. What would your father say?"

Rage billows up within me. Yes, I am king but Grall knows just how to make me feel like a child.

TWENTY-NINE

EVALIE

Thirty two paces. Yup. Still the same. I wish I didn't have to be back at my nervous pacing routine, but here we are. I think some ancient Earth human writer once said 'the course of love never did run smooth' and, by the stars, they were right.

But is this even love between Avirix and I? Because that's why I am pacing and I don't even know if love is the reason. It certainly wasn't made clear by our interactions today.

After I left his chamber early this morning (a lifetime ago!) I felt like everything between us was as certain as the ground beneath my feet. Sure, there are thorny details to work out like me being a low-life human and him being a King, but that had seemed to fade away into nothing as we kissed in the dawn light.

But, at lunch today, when he joined us, he seemed distant, not himself. Certainly not the open, giving lover from before. No matter how hard I tried, I couldn't read him. It was like a specter - every time I thought I had caught a glimpse of his real mood, it had slipped past me.

Any why should you care? You know what the situation is for him. For you both.

Yes, I am *well* aware of the political implications that would follow our...attachment. But last night meant so much. Could it not have meant the same to him as it did to me? Had I read it all wrong?

Pace. Pace. Pace.

Last night was unlike anything I'd ever felt before. And it all pointed me in one direction - falling in love with the King of the Plains. A fateful direction, indeed.

Pausing to listen, I am glad I don't hear one peep out of the twins. They were difficult to get to bed tonight and I really need the quiet and the space to think all this through.

What I'm really confused by is what to do next. Do I go to him this evening? Will he come to me? I don't know whether to stay or go - it's an awful feeling, like I'm adrift at sea.

How did I even get myself into this mess in the first place?

I'm going to wear a rut in the floor - even one as fancy as this one.

My thoughts are jolted back to reality when a harsh knock tears at my ears. Looking to the door, it practically vibrates with the pounding.

Nervously, I step over to answer it. Instantly, I regret this decision, but the knocking was not to be ignored.

Opening the door reveals three imposing figures. One, clad in robes and carrying a scepter, stood sandwiched between two Skuyr goons whom I vaguely recognize. But from where? And why would this high ranking Drokan be seen hanging out with Skuyr?

"Good evening. I believe you are the nanny?" The man

in the robes speaks, barely moving his mouth. It is deeply unsettling.

"I am," I reply, trying to keep the tremble out of my voice.

"Good." He turns to the goons. "She's all yours."

The Skuyr rush forward as I quickly back away. It's then, with a hollow shock, that I realize where I've seen these two before. They are Rrame's henchmen. I've seen them shaking down many a sad sack back at the village. Why are they here now and how can I get out of this as quickly as possible?

"Wait! What? What's going on? I—"

Two sets of strong, ropy arms soon pin me clumsily as I appeal to the official looking man in the middle.

"You make the King soft. Softness is weakness. And we can't have that. Especially not now."

I shake my head vigorously. I can't begin to understand what he's talking about. And how does he know about the king and I?

"I don't know what you mean...and who are you to control the king this way?" I don't know where I found the courage to spit out those words but they come out of me just the same. The Skuyr respond by gripping me tighter. I am starting to lose feeling in my lower arms.

A flash of pure anger criss-crosses the placid face of the robed man before me.

"You think yourself clever, do you? Putting forth ideas about 'fated mates' in his head? Ensuring you and your puny kind will be well taken care of by putting a lot of ancient bunk in his brain? Well, I'm here to assure you we don't need your meddling."

Fated mates? What is he talking about? I've never heard of such a thing. My head shakes once more.

The man's face peels back into a horrible grin.

"Ingenious of you to rustle up that old tradition. I'd forgotten it myself." He holds up a long, wizened finger. "And if you're wondering - I know because it is my business to know. My spies see all and tell *me* all. Which makes me quite powerful, if you couldn't tell."

None of this computes with me. But one thing is clear - Avirix is in danger. What would he say or do if he knew the extent to which he was being watched? I'm sure no king would want this - especially from one of his own?

"Please. Let me go. There's nothing between us—"

"Hush. We are way beyond bargaining. Besides, my spies have done their homework on you too, my dear. Seems there is a need for you back home. A much more pressing need than your services here and one that serves many parties."

Why couldn't this guy just get to the point?

"What?"

"Once you are married off to a certain dashing Skyur back home, where you belong, things will be much easier for all involved. Look at it this way - you'll be taken care of and you'll be *out of my way.*"

Suddenly, it all makes sense. A sickening, dreadful sense, but sense just the same. Rrame. He has set this ball in motion and has put himself up on the bargaining block to get me. And it's clear I have nothing to negotiate with.

"Let me go! The king won't stand for this!" I begin to struggle against the vile goons that hold me.

"What the king doesn't know won't hurt him. You should go back to where you belong." With that, the robed man turned his back to me and barked, "Keep her alive but subdue her as you please. Just make sure she is delivered in one piece. I owe your...boss that much."

With that, he leaves. That's when utter panic courses through me and I begin to thrash. With a fury I didn't know I have, I buck and flail against the goons.

I hear swearing and grunts as they try to bring me to heel. But I won't allow it.

I simply won't. I need to get to the King. I need to get to my...fated mate?

The idea drops in, like oil on water and it's the one moment of clarity I have before everything goes utterly and completely black.

THIRTY
AVIRIX

With a decisive shove, I push my goblet of wine away. While I usually enjoy this treat at the end of a long day, tonight the *kishkesh,* a wine made from a blend of *jyranth* grapes and light shone through crystals, helps me unwind.

But tonight, nothing helps. I'm too antsy. Too consumed with my feelings for Evalie - and the knowledge that she doesn't quite know their depths yet. And yet she must. I must tell her about our fated mate connection. The longer we are apart, the more the need grows.

But, I know that once I tell her, there is no going back. My entire future, both as King and as her mate, hangs in a tenuous balance. That is, if I can find any such balance at all. I know that my kingdom, and most especially my most conservative advisors, will have many feelings on the subject.

Grall's gaunt face rises in my mind's eye, taking away my pleasure at thinking of Evalie. I banish the thoughts and concentrate on something I might do instead. Perhaps, by doing, I can whisk away these anxieties.

Go to her. Explain it all. She will reciprocate.

I want to believe this. But, after lunch today, I was not so sure. It's true, I was a bit distant, and we cannot be as affectionate as we like in front of the twins just yet, but I couldn't help but think that perhaps last night was merely an aberration.

No. Nothing that felt that good, or so perfect, could be an aberration.

The words of the priest Ziw come to mind, soothing me like no glass of *kishkesh* could.

To complete the fated mate bond, he had explained, each mate must accept the bond. They must *submit* to it.

To me, submission was as easy as falling into a pool of warm water. I only hoped Evalie would feel the same.

But, whatever she felt, she had a right to know. She had a right to choose. No fated mate should be isolated from such precious information.

The night was drawing on and I knew I could find her alone in the nursery. The twins would long be asleep. I had been aching for her all day but so much had constrained against us.

The largest constraint is her consent. Get it now. Go.

My chair scraped along the floor as I stood up, causing my jaw to clench. Only Evalie could ease my tensions now. I just hope that she feels as I do. Deep down, I know she does.

As I reach for my office door, I am surprised to see the door open in towards me. Who could be visiting me at such an hour?

Grall's form quickly answers my question and I swallow hard, placing my kingly mask over my worried features. What does he want and why now? This had better be pressing.

"Your Majesty," he intoned, his voice grating my nerves, "I am sorry to intrude but I wanted to bring something alarming to your attention..."

"Yes? What?" Why is he making me work so damn hard? Just spit out the information, man!

"Of course. Well, I happened to pass the nursery door just now and I noticed...well, quite a din."

"A din? Explain." I wave a hand at him. What could be wrong at the nursery?

"Yes, sire. It seems that the children are very much awake and, from what I can tell, are *unattended*. The nanny, at least in my estimation, is not present."

A small stone of dread lands squarely in my stomach. As I hear Grall's words, the stone begins to expand and grow. Swallowing once more, I refuse to let panic overtake me. But where could Evalie possibly be?

"I thought....she might be in your presence, sire, so I paid you a call. But, as we both plainly see, she is not here. I fear I don't know where else she may be. Perhaps—"

I don't wait to hear the rest of his sentence. Pushing past him, I tear out of the office and barrel down the hallway towards the nursery.

She is there. She has to be. He is hearing things. Things that are not true. She will be there. She will look at me and laugh at my foolishness.

Soon, I find myself at the nursery door. Even before I open it, I hear the wailing within. Or's shrill voice overtakes that of his sister, but both are clearly scared and alone.

The door is unlocked and I enter it within seconds. Like a dam opening, the children, standing in the middle of the room, take one look at me and rush full speed into my legs.

"Hey, hey there. What's all the fuss? Did you both have a bad dream?" I put my arms awkwardly around them (though less so than before) and kneel to face them directly.

"We...woke...up...alone..." Or says, between sobs.

"Scary, so scary," Tali whispers, her hair askew and her eyes wide with abject terror.

"Shhhh, it's all right now. I'm here. There's nothing to be scared of. Where's Evalie?"

I know it's a silly question. But a part of me will not succumb to the idea that she's not there. This is all just a farce, a joke, nothing more.

"Gone!" Or wails, louder than before. Tali merely looks at me and nods.

"Let me just check, all right? Will you walk with me?"

They both nod and follow me like small ducklings. Doing my best not to move like a man in pure panic, I move from room to room in the nursery suite, checking for any signs of Evalie.

Nothing. Not a trace.

The last place I look, her closet, makes the stone in my stomach grow to the size of a boulder.

Gone. Her bags, her belongings. Everything that would indicate she had ever been here. All missing. All taken.

The children, sensing that something has happened to change the tension in the room, cling to me with a ferocity that mirrors my inward feelings.

"It's all right. We just have to find out where Ms Evalie went. She will turn up soon, I promise."

My words sound hollow and forced. In response, the children burrow their heads into my legs once more. Their sniffling is muffled but constant.

Where is she? Where could she have gone? *Why* would she possibly leave? And why now?

The questions swirling within me threaten to loosen my

hold on the situation. I must hold it together for the sake of the twins.

Sensing movement just beyond the nursery door, I see Grall prowling about - a virulent onlooker.

Make him at least useful then.

"Grall. Come to me."

The advisor comes to my side with a swiftness that is remarkable for someone of his age.

"Evalie is gone. Search for her. High and low. She simply must be returned."

His beady eyes, for just a moment, bore into me with a frankness that was not there a second before.

"For the sake of the children, of course," I stutter.

His beady look vanishes, replaced by a mask of concern.

"Right away, sire. For the sake of the children."

He swoops out of the nursery and I hold the children to me. It's unclear who is comforting who.

THIRTY-ONE

EVALIE

I wake up in darkness. Even with no light to see by, I know I'm somewhere I've never been beyond. The very walls — wherever they are — radiate strangeness. *This is not a good place.*

My subconscious knows before I do. I blink, straining to see something, anything to tell me where I am, before I remember. Everything comes flooding back to me, with the brute force of a tsunami.

That horrible advisor. The Skuyr gang members. Fighting as hard as I could, then the world going black.

Rrame.

The convenient Skuyr who wants me? That can only be one person, even if his gang members hadn't been the ones to abduct me. Wherever I am, I'm in Rrame's power.

The realization forces the breath from of my lungs. I gasp, sucking in the stale air of my prison, but I can't seem to get enough. I'm panicking.

I'm panicking, and there's a dull ache in my head. I feel an itch down my temple. My hands are bound, so I can't scratch it, which is probably good. I'm betting if I touched my head, I'd find blood.

That thought doesn't help me. The panic gets worse, my heart seemingly trying to fight its way out of my ribcage. I cough in my effort to just get enough *air*.

The door swings open.

Light filters into the room, chasing away at least a little of my agitation. Being able to see is a signal to my brain that all is not lost, I suppose.

But it is.

Because who is coming through that doorway, but Rrame.

He flicks on a lamp, and I wince as brightness explodes across my eyes. I grit my teeth, trying not to show my discomfort, and focus my woozy gaze on Rrame's face. He wears a sickly smile, the kind that makes me want to slap him.

I push away the panic as best I can, and straighten. If Rrame thinks he can have his way with me without a fight, he's dead wrong.

"My darling," he croons, in a nauseating slime of a voice. "My beautiful soon-to-be-wife. Are you excited for our nuptials tomorrow? You may have any kind of cake you ask for, you know."

"Shut it, Rrame." I practically spit at him. "You know I'll never marry you, you scumbag. You had to resort to kidnapping me just to get me to talk to you! Pathetic."

As I knew he would, Rrame flips in a second. His falsely tender expression vanishes, replacing by a nasty snarl.

"Bitchy today, aren't we?" he hisses. "So sorry your plan to trap a King didn't work, and that you'll have to marry me instead."

I'm not fast enough to keep my feelings off my face.

Rrame's words shock me all too easily... and spark the beginnings of a painful longing for Avirix.

"Oh yes," he sneers. "I heard all about it directly from the palace. Thought you could fuck your way into a crown, didn't you? Well tough. You'll have to settle for Queen of the Slums, by my side."

"Do you have mold in your ears?" I manage to sneer back. "Did you not hear me? I'll *never* marry you."

"Ah, that's where you're wrong." Rrame begins to circle me, lazily vicious, like a predator. "See, I have your mother, and I won't hesitate to get rid of the old bitch if you refuse me."

"What?" I whisper. I immediately wish I could swallow the terrified word, but Rrame pounces in.

"That's right. Tomorrow morning you'll marry me, saying every single word you're supposed to. Either you gain a husband, or you lose a mother. Your choice, my *dearest*. But forgive me if I'm hoping you choose to have me on your hands, rather than spilled blood."

With a final lascivious flick of his tongue on his bottom lip, Rrame leaves. He turns out the light as he goes, and that does it.

Sobs well up in my throat as my mind spirals back into utter panic. Panic, and despair. I collapse to the floor, my bones sapped of strength by the future before me.

Of course I'll do anything to save my mother's life. It's not even a question but... the horrible truth is that even if Avirix finds out what happens and comes for me, I'll already be married.

Married, and trapped.

Whether or not there actually is anything to my relationship with Avirix, any chance we had will be cut off. Drokan so rarely divorce that it would be an impossible scandal for Avirix to be with someone who'd already been married.

As if me being human weren't bad enough.

Perhaps Avirix will come for me anyway. I know he cares enough about me to not want a life of misery for me — and that's what I face as Rrame's wife. He may rescue me, reinstate me as the kids' nanny perhaps.

We could never be together but at least I'd be near him, and still with Or and Tali.

The frantic whirling of my brain shrieks a dozen reasons while all of this is stupid. Avirix won't come for me, how in the stars could he find me? It would take weeks, weeks a King doesn't have. Besides, no one would want a Skuyr's former wife anywhere near royal children.

My shredded thoughts seize on that: royal children. Or and Tali's sweet faces float in my head, and my tears come harder. I taste salt on my lips as I weep, understanding I may never see them again.

Them, or Avirix.

Now that the possibility is gone, I finally see what I truly wanted, deep down. I wanted to make a family, with Or and Tali and Avirix. I wanted food fights with them, and dinners in the garden, and storytelling, and silly games.

I wanted togetherness. I wanted love.

Waves of mourning for the life I'll never have crash through me. Dropping my head against the cold musty floor, I let myself cry.

Tomorrow, I must be strong, but tonight, I can only grieve.

THIRTY-TWO

AVIRIX

I dream, of nothing in particular. Shapes and colors, and the sense of happiness. My subconscious must know Or and Tali are snuggled in my arms, as they're in every dream I manage to catch a wisp of.

Then, the wisps eddy away as an unpleasant voice breaks through my slumber.

"Your majesty? King Avirix?"

I blink to wakefulness. The warm solid shapes of the twins thankfully don't fade away with the rest of my dreams. I continue to hold them to me, as I take in Grall standing in the center of the nursery.

Who knew, that these little ones would bring me so much comfort.

"Ah... my King," repeats Grall, eying the children snoring on my chest. "I have news."

He pauses, probably waiting for me to disentangle myself from the children.

Well, I don't plan to.

"What news, Grall?" I ask crisply. "Don't keep me in suspense."

"My apologies," replies my advisor, too unctuously for my liking. "I merely wished to tell you intelligence has located the children's nanny."

"Where is she?" I sit bolt upright, dislodging the children despite my intentions to the contrary. Luckily, they are dead to the world and sleep on.

"It seems she ran off to marry her Skuyr lover." Grall sniffs. "Intelligence located her at his house, with nuptials planned for today. Although why she had to leave secretly in the dead of night instead of simply resigning, I just don't know."

My jaw drops, and I feel a low trembling in my spine. With a few sentences, Grall has turned my entire world inside out.

Evalie... ran off? Evalie has a lover? She's... getting married?

"Humans," sighs Grall, shaking his head. "Always behaving like trash, even when there's no reason to."

"You're sure of this?" I hear myself rumble. I extricate myself from the kids and walk to stand directly in front of my advisor. "You're *certain*?"

"My lord...?" Grall turns confused eyes on me. "Why would I tell you if I wasn't certain? Would you like to see the images captured by Intelligence?"

My stomach turns over with revulsion at the idea. See images of Evalie — the woman I'd thought was my *zalshagri* — in the arms of another?

"No," I choke out. "Thank you for informing me."

For a moment, I see what looks like a flash of satisfaction in Grall's eyes. The next second, it's gone, replaced with mild sadness.

"Let me know if I can help you hire a new nanny, my King." He shakes his head one last time, and leaves.

I stand like I've been struck in the face.

Or stabbed in the gut.

That is what it feels like. Like someone ripped my vi-blade from my nerveless fingers and buried it in my flesh.

It hurts, to my core.

All the times I should've known rush into my head. Evalie defended the Skuyr, for Krodo's sake! After they attacked her and the children! Or was that fake the whole time? Could her lover be a Skuyr rebel?

I shake my head in fury. It was right in front of me. And here I thought Evalie was an idealist!

She IS, says a voice in my head. *She would never lie to you.*

My fists clench, and I try to dispel such stupidity from my mind. She DID lie to me. I bet that time she visited her mother was a lie! She was likely visiting this lover of hers — after all, she refused the Convei, and my escort. She didn't want me to see where she was actually going.

I let out a huge, agonized howl. I can't help myself. Anger and pain are tearing me apart from the inside. I lurch towards a trinket standing innocently on a shelf. With a single swipe, I send it crashing to the floor.

"Uncle...?" A high voice asks behind me, and I whirl.

The children. What am I going to tell them?

"Are you mad?" Or's eyes are big. "Why you mad?"

"Where's Evalie?" Tali's question is a new dagger to my heart. "Evalie helps you not be mad."

"Evalie..." I hiss, then stop myself. I try to make my voice more measured. "Evalie is why I'm mad. She left us."

Tali's brows furrow and Or crosses his arms.

"She would never," says Tali.

"Prolly lost," adds Or. His eyes grow even bigger. "We gotta find her!"

"No!" I bark. I can't seem to stop the acid words falling from my lips. "She's left us. She abandoned us. She abandoned YOU!"

"No." Or seems unbothered by my outburst. He lifts himself off the couch and walks towards me. "Evalie stays with us. We know." He touches his heart. "We feel it."

I stare at him. I don't know what to say. How do I explain a lie as big as Evalie's to a three year old?

"Here," says Tali, following her brother but going a bit further, coming right up to me. She places her hand on her heart. "We feel it. She loves us."

"Then why..." I begin to ask, but Tali isn't done.

"Don't you feel?" She moves her hand from her heart to my own. "What does this part say? Did Evalie go?"

At Tali's touch, the rage drains out of my body. I blink at her, as Or comes to join his sister. He places his hand on top of hers, and I realize — I do sense something internally. It's not anger, it's... distress. Grief.

And not my own.

It's Evalie's.

My jaw clenches. There's only one reason Evalie would be feeling like this.

She's been taken against her will!

I leap to my feet, away from the children.

"You're right," I tell them, my heart pounding. "I was wrong. So, so, wrong. Evalie is lost, I have to go find her!"

I seize the connection I'm feeling. As much as it wounds me to feel this level of distress from my Evalie, I must focus on it.

As I do, I feel myself pulled in a very specific direction — the direction of Evalie's old neighborhood. In an instant, I run out to the balcony, leaping into the air. I'm all set to shoot off to where I feel Evalie, until I hear a tiny grunt behind me.

Or is laboring an arm's length off the floor of the balcony, his half-grown wings straining like mad. He's trying as hard as he can to take off, just like me.

My heart melts, and I swoop back down to the balcony, catching Or in my arms. I bring him back to solid ground, and hold him tight.

"You stay here, with your sister," I tell him, catching sight of Tali peering through the doors. I smile at her, and hold out my hand. She rushes into my arms too. "I promise both of you. I'll return soon — with Evalie. I swear it."

THIRTY-THREE

EVALIE

I feel like I'm going to throw up.

Standing next to Rrame at the altar is something out of my worst nightmares. Perhaps even beyond them — I'm not sure even my nightmares could've come up with this.

We're in a small, dimly lit room, that smells of mildew. I'm in a sham of a wedding outfit, a torn and grimy ceremonial star cloak hanging around my shoulders. A legal clerk with a pinched face and a leering mouth is spreading out the marriage contract. Rrame's gang members lounge against the walls.

And in the corner is Mar. Not beaming at me and trying to hide her misty eyes like she would be at my actual wedding. No, she's gagged with a dirty rag and tied up so tightly she can barely move.

Seeing my mother that way sickens me. It rips long jagged claws into my heart. And as Rrame intended, it reminds me why I'm standing here so docilely. Even though I'm beginning to be certain I'd rather die than marry Rrame.

I could. I could go through with this farce, but then jump in front of a Buzz.

It's a horribly seductive thought. I'd have spared Mar by legally binding myself to Rrame, but my death would keep him from ever truly possessing me.

I can't leave my mother, though. For one, I can't cause her that grief. For another, Rrame is exactly the kind of vindictive bastard who would murder Mar out of pique for losing me.

As if Rrame can hear the way my thoughts are tending, he leans in next to me. His hot, foul breath blasts my face.

"I'm so looking forward to our lifetime of happiness," he rasps, sadistic glee underlying his every word. "I think your mother should live with us, don't you? So I can keep an eye on her."

And keep me in line by continuing to threaten her.

I refuse to reply. Instead I keep my eyes trained forward, stoically waiting for the clerk to begin the proceedings.

In the end, I don't have to wait long. Rrame only has time to pour a few more sentences of bile in my ear, before the shifty clerk clears his throat.

"Friends, we are gathered here to witness the joining of Rrame Szandrol and Evalie Martin. May I confirm at least three witnesses?"

Each of Rrame's gang members give a loud grunt, one by one. It would be comical, if it weren't another step towards my doom.

"More than three, excellent." The clerk grins nastily. "Now, this is a remarkable union, a Skuyr and a human brought together by love."

I can't help it. I make a choking noise deep in my throat. The idea that the pure, beautiful emotion I feel for Mar, for

ATHENA STORM

Or and Tali, for Avirix — the idea THAT is at all related to the reason I'm marrying Rrame?

It's obscene.

Rrame jams a sharp elbow into my side, and tips his head at one of his minions, who goes to stand next to Mar. I get the message.

"May this marriage be blessed by Kincaid the Clever, and by the Faraway Stars," continues the clerk, who seems amused by my revulsion. "Now, Evalie Martin, do you, of your own free will and with celestial light in your heart, choose to bind yourself to Rrame Szandrol?"

Those are just the rote words of a human wedding, but hearing them stabs me. My eyes fill with tears, even as I try to move my mouth in a single horrid lie — '*yes.*' My mother's life depends on it.

Before I can form the syllable that will ruin me, there's a gigantic crash. I whirl around, fearing Mar has already paid for my hesitation.

Instead, I see a miracle.

I see Avirix.

He's sent the door flying clean out of its frame, crashing directly into one of Rrame's men. Using his wings to gain some height, Avirix smashes down on the solid sheet of metal, crushing the gang member beneath it.

"KILL HIM!" bellows Rrame, shocking me.

Does he really think he can get away with killing the King of Plains?

Apparently, he does. The remaining four of his men rush at Avirix, phasers and knives already drawn. One squeezes off a well-aimed shot, but too late. My King is already moving.

Remarkably agile for such a brawny man, he spins around the line of fire and into two of the minions. A vee of a blade I didn't see at first emerges in the palm of his hand, and he stabs one Skuyr in the gut with it, then the other.

Each one lets out a gurgling howl, and slumps to the ground. Avirix turns, ready to take on the other two, but one has already jumped on his back. Avirix roars, twisting and flapping to try to get Rrame's lackey OFF.

I lurch towards him, needing to help, but Rrame's thin fingers snatch my arm. He drags me into him, and I yelp, immobilized by his grip.

Avirix is still trying to get the Skuyr off his back, while the other one slashes at his torso. Out of the corner of my eye, I see that Mar has fallen to the floor. At first the sight makes me wail, but then I realize — she's inching towards the fallen henchmen.

Wiggling strategically, she pushes herself against the knife of one of the dead men. Her bonds are tight, but must not be very strong, as she saws only briefly before the narrow ropes fall away. Joy fills me as she gets to her feet, wrenching the gag out of her mouth.

"Run, Mar!" I cry. "Get out of here!"

"Are you kidding?" she tosses at me, as she picks up a chair. I watch wide-eyed as she waits until Avirix's attacker-laden back is to her. Rrame snarls and lets go of me, rushing for Mar, but he's too late.

She slams the chair into the attacker's spine. He screams and falls to the ground. In seconds Rrame is nearly at my mother's throat — but now that he's freed, Avirix gets there first.

With a growl of deep hatred, he interposes himself between Mar and Rrame. The gang leader hisses and raises his phaser, but again, he's too slow.

Faster than I can process, Avirix has already buried his vi-blade into Rrame's neck.

Yellowish blood bubbles up from the wound, as Rrame staggers backward. He can't speak, can't do anything except grab at his shredded throat.

And then, he falls to the floor.

Dead.

A relief I never wanted to feel at the death of another living being fills me. I drop to my knees sobbing, as the clerk and Rrame's one remaining minion sprint out the door.

Warm arms go around me, pulling me into a solid and comforting chest. Avirix cradles me to him, pressing his face into my air. He holds me tightly, but he's shaking.

"Evalie, my Evalie," he murmurs. "I can't believe I almost lost you. You're everything to me. You're my *zalshagri*."

THIRTY-FOUR

AVIRIX

F inally saying the word *zalshagri* aloud to Evalie makes the air chime. She must feel it too, because she raises her head and looks at me with wonder.

"*Zalshagri*," she repeats slowly, the word sounding impossibly beautiful in her mouth. "Avirix... what does that mean?"

"It means fated mate," I tell her, my pulse racing with love and adrenaline. "It means... well." I take a deep breath, and reach for Ziw's words. "All living things are connected on Genesis, by a sacred life energy. As a pair of *zalshagri*, we are connected even more deeply. We are destined to be together, by Krodo and the Stars themselves."

Evalie looks deep into my eyes, her hand reaching out to cup my jaw.

"Even as you were explaining it, I already knew," she murmurs. "I feel like I've known it all my life. *Zalshagri*."

It's then that I realize the connection I tracked to find her was new. Before the children made me listen for it, I'd never sensed it. Perhaps that could be my own stupidity but perhaps... something changed.

Evalie must have accepted the bond somehow. As Ziw said, for the *zalshagri* union to be complete, both mates must accept the truth in their hearts. If Evalie acknowledged her feelings for me, that would explain how I could find her so magically.

That's almost enough. Almost enough for me to put aside all my hesitations and believe that Evalie feels the same way that I do. But I need to hear it.

"Evalie, I love you. Greater than love, I am feel joined to you by the most pure and holy force of our planet. Do you... do you...?"

"Feel the same way?" As always, my Evalie takes mercy on me. A sun-filled smile bursts onto her face, before she throws her arms around my neck. "Of course I do. Avirix, I love you so much."

The greatest happiness I've ever known suffuses me. I put my hands on either side of Evalie's face and pull her back, so I can gaze at her perfection.

Naturally then gazing isn't nearly enough, so I kiss her.

It's better than even the kisses we shared the other night. With the fullness of the *zalshagri* bond between us, I can feel her love and pleasure radiating back to me. I know just where to touch her and she knows just how to slide her lips over mine to drive me wild.

We could kiss for hours, I think, but a loud clearing of the throat interrupts us.

Reluctantly, I pull back from Evalie. Her lips are swollen and her eyes sparkling, which almost tugs me right back in. Yet I'm not given time to.

"I'm really very touched by this," says Evalie's mother matter-of-factly. "Loving and appreciating my daughter definitely endears you to me, King of the Plains. But can we leave the gang headquarters, before more Skuyr show up?"

Evalie bursts out laughing, surprising me.

"Mar," she says affectionately, jumping to her feet and rushing to embrace her mother. "You're right, you're always right. And you were *amazing*."

"Indeed you were," I observe, stiffly. I get to my feet, and give my mate's mother a shallow bow. "Your bravery delivered me from a difficult situation."

"And don't you forget it," retorts Mar, but with a smile that belies the saltiness of her words.

Suddenly though, the smile slides away. She disentangles herself from her daughter's arms, with a distracted kiss on Evalie's forehead. Stalking to me, she practically pokes me in the chest.

"So are you going to marry my Evalie, King Avirix?" A skeptical look has now utterly replaced that momentary smile. "I was eavesdropping and I won't apologize for it. *Zalsha*-whatever, fated mate hooey, it doesn't mean shit if you hide her away. Are you going to be ashamed that you're 'mated' to a human?"

I blink at her. The thought had literally never, ever crossed my mind. Even before I knew that my relationship with Evalie was genuinely divine, I never imagined hiding away the woman I love.

I couldn't.

I open my mouth to say so, but Evalie is speaking.

"There's already opposition, you know," she mutters, an angry blush rising up her neck. She meets my eyes, and I see she doesn't doubt me. There's something else going on, which she quickly elucidates. "I ended up here thanks to your advisor. The one with the scepter and the breastplate. He gave me to Rrame to get rid of me as a *temptation* for you."

"GRALL DID WHAT?" My fists clench of their own

accord, and my blood runs hot. "That slimy, double-cross-ing, evil old man. He will pay. I will MAKE HIM pay."

"Good, good, you do that," puts in Evalie's mother. "Maybe let me watch. But my question still stands — are you going to marry my girl?"

Breathing deeply, I subdue the surge of bloodthirsty rage that wants to send me directly to the palace to destroy Grall. There is something more important here. I can deal with Grall later.

"I am," I tell my love's only parent solemnly. Taking a single long step, I go to Evalie and sink to my knees in front of her. "Evalie, it would be the greatest honor and happiness of my life if you would consent to marry me."

Tears jump into her eyes as she nods, the sweetest smile on her lips. She knows what *zalshagri* means now, so she isn't surprised by my proposal, I think. She is, however, as thrilled as I am at the prospect of a shared life together, joined in all things.

"I promise you," I say, with a quick nod to her mother. "I promise both of you. No matter what, I will make my *zalshagri* my Queen — for all to see."

THIRTY-FIVE

EVALIE

It is the day of my wedding, and I can scarcely believe it.

So much has happened to bring my Avirix and me to this day. The most important of which was a tearful reunion with Or and Tali.

The twins clung to me for hours after Avirix brought me and Mar back to the palace. I think if they hadn't missed Mar too, they would've clung to me for days. Instead, they transferred to her for a bit, then to Avirix, then back to me.

In bits and pieces, I got the whole story about the twins helping Avirix see through Grall's lies. Even thinking about it now, I get tears in my eyes. I understand why Avirix was so doubtful — wasn't I, at so many moments? But the fact that our little ones saved both of us, well... it's something to cherish forever.

There were other, more intense events, too. Grall was swiftly tried and imprisoned. I think even those of Avirix's advisors that are horrified at the idea of a human queen couldn't quite condone treason to the crown. To a one, they condemned Grall to wither his life away in a cold cell.

Riding the wave of Grall's disgrace, Avirix was able to push forward his new edicts for Pilger. He changed things so that the farmers of the region actually own their land, even if they still have to rent equipment from Skuyr and Drokan lenders. It's not all that should happen, but it was a start — and an important enough one that the rebellion faded away.

Most recently, there was the terrifying public announcement of our *zalshagri* bond, thankfully crafted and overseen by a priest Avirix brought in. Ziw, his name is, and everything about him sets me at ease. I think hearing of the bond from the Reider's lips helped many a Drokan accept the deep meaning of my love for Avirix and his for me.

Of course, there are still naysayers. I can't count the number of sidelong glances and sneers I get anytime we're among Drokan nobles. Until Avirix set up a filter on my Misiv, I was even getting horrid messages from people who want me to 'release our King from your evil spells.'

It's been a busy and stressful ten-days, but most of that slips away as Mar takes my arm.

We're standing at the end of a long pathway, a carpet of soft moss and grass. I'm sheathed in a sumptuous sapphire blue gown, the color of wedding dress only royalty may wear. In a nod to my human traditions, a ceremonial star cloak embroidered with precious crystals tumbles down my back.

As Mar takes my arm and begins to walk me down the aisle, my eyes find Avirix. He stands waiting, looking impossibly handsome in his own sapphire blue wedding garb. His wings arch out behind him, as is Drokan tradition, reminding me of that blissful first night we flew beneath the stars.

Behind him, there's a gorgeous blossoming tree. Its white and gold blooms nod, giving off a delicate scent that seems oddly familiar. Ziw brought it with him, to bless our marriage. I never thought it would actually take root and flourish here, but it really did.

I realize I'm overwhelmed. All these thoughts are my attempt to hold onto my surroundings, and stay calm. I'm trying not to look to either side of me, since I know what I'll find.

Humans in the audience, what a symbol of change. I'm so happy and proud Avirix invited my people.

Yet alongside the humans, scowling advisors and wealthy Drokan families, radiating their displeasure at this unorthodox union.

How could I not be nervous?

I manage to get to my *zalshagri*'s side, the steady presence of my mother guiding me all the way. Pressing a kiss to my temple, Mar murmurs in my ear.

"I'm so happy for you, my girl. You've found someone worthy of you."

I squeeze her hand as she turns away, and I catch the telltale glint of tears in her eyes.

I knew she would get emotional. She's as soft a touch as I am, deep down.

Mar joins Or and Tali, who are all dressed up and looking very fancy. Yakwa stands with them, a hand on each of their shoulders. I sneak them a little wave, and get twin sunbeam smiles back in response.

At last, I turn to Avirix. His face is a balm to my raw nerves, soothing me at least a little. So is Ziw's smile, gentle and as warm as a blanket on a winter's day.

"Today we are blessed to witness the joining of the first *zalshagri* pair in centuries," he begins, his clear deep voice carrying over all attending. "To be *zalshagri* is a divine gift, from Krodo who shaped us all, and from the holiness that came from the Faraway Stars."

His words resonate in my bones, once again stating to the world the thing I know to be true.

Avirix and I belong together, now and for eternity.

Even with that certainty, listening to Ziw begin the official ceremony of joining is nerve-wracking. I'm anxious that someone will stand up, and yell that this is all a disgrace. That wouldn't stop us, but it would hurt.

"Now, Avirix, King of the Plains Drokan, and Evalie Martin, daughter of humans and the Faraway Stars, please touch the Soul Tree, and hear the words of joining."

I exchange a loving glance with my *zalshagri*, and as one we reach out and touch the blossoming tree.

My fingers land on the smooth bark, and it's like a pleasant energy shock goes up my arm. Without looking at him, I know Avirix is feeling the same thing.

Like a cool bath, a sense of perfect calm washes over me. My nervousness, all my anxieties, they simply sluice away. For a moment, I can see the entirety of Genesis, connected by threads of glowing green light.

At the center of a small pool of those threads, stand me and Avirix. I can't explain it, but all at once I'm given complete and utter clarity.

Here, next to this man, on this day, is exactly where I was always meant to be.

"Good night Or," I say to the sleepy little boy, wrapping him in my arms. "You were so good today."

"Me too!" demands Tali, wriggling out of Evalie's embrace. She sticks her head under my elbow, pushing her way into my arms alongside Or. "Also I was good today!"

"So you were," I agree, chuckling and planting at kiss on top of her head. "Both of you were wonderful."

"You really were," observes Evalie, looking at my group hug fondly. "That was a lot of feasting and dancing even for me! And it was my wedding!"

"I like feasting," Tali informs us. "NOT dancing."

"Dancing is fun!" objects Or, waking up a little. He lurches out of my arms and executes a hilarious spin move, collapsing into Evalie's waiting hands.

"Then we'll do more, but tomorrow." She stands him on his feet, and rubs between his wings. "For now, bedtime."

"Yes, bedtime!" Ya-ya's familiar voice joins us. She stands hands on her hips, smiling at our family scene. "Your parents have said good night to you, now off we go!"

Parents?

I think about that for a moment. Technically I am the twins' uncle and Evalie is their... stepmom? I dismiss those empty words from my mind. Ya-ya is right. Whatever the precise terms are, Evalie and I are Or and Tali's parents.

And we are proud to be.

With one last hug and kiss for each of them, Evalie and I get to our face, holding hands. The tired children willingly stumble to Ya-ya, who puts her capable hands on their heads.

"Come come, the sooner we wash our faces the sooner we can be snoring." My former nanny turns to me, a glint in her eye. "Good night, my King, my Queen. Enjoy... your evening."

She sends me a wink, and I nearly choke. I can't tell if it's hilarious or disconcerting that the woman who cared for me as a child is now being suggestive about my wedding night.

I decide it doesn't matter. What matters is getting that wedding night started, and soon. Going with impulse, I sweep Evalie into my arms. She lets out a gasp of delighted surprise, as I stride to the balcony.

The doors are already open to let in the cool night air, so it's the matter of a thought to lift off into the air. With slow, steady beats of my wings, I take us around our palace to the balcony of my room. Hovering for a minute, I turn so we can both see our realm spread out beneath us.

Besiel glimmers, its riot of lights fading towards the peripheries. Dark grassland and hills are barely visible in the distance, yet I catch a glimpse of a shining lake — the heavens replicated on the earth.

"I would say this is even more beautiful than our first night together." Evalie sighs with contentment, leaning her head against my chest. "But I don't think anything will ever be more beautiful than the moment I could finally believe you might have feelings for me."

"I'll never forget," I murmur to her, as I touch down gently on the balcony. "I didn't know except as an ache deep in my soul, but I was already lost in love with you then."

"Oh, Avirix." Evalie goes on her tiptoes, and kisses me. "Even not knowing, you made me so, so happy."

"And I look forward to a lifetime of continuing to do so," I tell her. "You know... I wanted to make sure you know how much you've changed me. That night, and every night since, and every day since I met you."

"Changed you?" Evalie raises one slender eyebrow. "Avirix, I love you just as you are."

"It's not that I'm a different man, it's that I'm a wiser one. A better one." I take her hand. "All the times you challenged me to think more about all my people, the Skuyr and the humans in addition to the Drokan. I'll never be an idealist like you, but you've opened my mind."

"It means so much to me that you hear me," breathes Evalie. "You have a noble heart, my love. Because you are a truly good man, you trust that I have only everyone's well-being in mind."

"I do. And because of that, I'll be a stronger and worthier King with you at my side." I hesitate. It's not exactly wedding night conversation, but I've been waiting to tell her all day. "In fact, I'm electing a human to the advisor vacancy left by Grall. For the first time, the Plains will have a human weighing in on policy."

"You have? You did!" Evalie throws her arms around my neck, pressing her entire body against mine. "That's wonderful! That's — that's — I didn't even mention that!"

"I can come up with things on my own, you know," I inform her, with wry affection.

"I know." She draws back, and strokes my cheekbone. "But I do hope you're ready for me to keep challenging you."

"Oh, I am." Deciding I'm done with the intellectual stuff, for the second time that night I sweep Evalie into my arms. "On every level."

She takes my meaning, her eyes flashing with desire and mischief. As I carry her into our bedroom, I nearly fall to my knees at the touch of her clever fingers exploring my waistband.

"Evalie," I groan.

In response, her fingers dip lower, as she begins raining soft, sensuous kisses onto my neck. I can barely stagger to the bed, so overcome am I with heat and need.

Another challenge, indeed.

At last I make it, spilling my love onto our bed. She looks impossibly beautiful, in her sapphire wedding gown, her cheeks flushed with happy pink, and her russet hair tumbling over her shoulders.

I lean down to kiss her. As my lips brush hers, she whispers softly,

"I was made for you, my love, my mate."

My heart swells for the millionth time that day.

"And I for you, Evalie. My *zalshagri*."

Then, I kiss her, and lose myself in everything we are, together.

THIRTY-SEVEN
EVALIE

Avirix and I have been together many times since we acknowledged the bond between us. There was no reason to not spend our nights as one, when our relationship itself is already scandalous enough.

Night after night, we couldn't keep our hands off each other. No matter how tired, or how difficult a day it had been, we *wanted* each other.

We want each other now, but somehow it's different. It's deeper, more meaningful, which I wouldn't have thought possible.

Perhaps it's the result of being sworn to each other, in front of Drokans and humans alike. Perhaps it's from having kind and wise Ziw sanctifying our love for each other.

Or maybe... maybe it's because we touched the Soul Tree together. I haven't asked Avirix what he felt then, because I already know. In that moment, we were one. A single entity, destined to find peace and bliss.

I feel that swell of rightness and contentment now. I burn for Avirix, as he trails kisses down my neck. My hips buck up to meet him, as he undoes my dress, one careful button by the next. Yet it's a more serene flame, like the steady light that burns all night long in a temple.

We're beyond words. We move like we can anticipate each other, and I suppose we can. I peel Avirix's shirt off him, he shrugs his shoulders so I can tug it down his arms. I run my hands over his deliciously firm chest, and he feathers his thumb over the curve of my breast.

We gasp in unison, the fire between us growing brighter.

But, we take our time. Once all our clothes are gone, our limbs entwine on top of our cushioned bed. My hands want to touch every rippling inch of him, trace the arcs of his wings, draw down along his angles.

We explore each other like it's the first time, for what feels like hours. Avirix discovers new corners of me that thrill to his touch — the soft skin behind my ear, the bottom of my shoulder blade, the sensitive skin behind my knees.

I feel like I'm being worshipped, and I feel like a worshipper at the same time.

The coals of our desire grow white hot, as heat consumes us. When the need suddenly overwhelms us both, we're taken by surprise. I'm nipping at the powerful muscle between Avirix's neck and shoulder, as he traces circles around my taut nipple — until all at once I have to have so, so much *more*.

We act in tandem.

In a single smooth motion, Avirix rolls me on top of him as I plunge myself down on his stiff cock. I cry out, as he gets out nothing but a strangled moan.

"Evalie," he manages to say, before I start to move.

"Avirix," I reply, and nothing else is necessary. Our names contain our entire world.

I can feel the delicious fullness of having my love inside

me forever, but also my body screams for me to take my pleasure.

Unable to resist, I begin to rock, back and forth on Avirix's hardness. He's stretching me to the breaking point, the perfect edge. And yet, I can feel him opening me further and further, each time I push my hips against his.

One of his huge, lightly calloused palms finds my breast, and I moan. Catching my nipple between his thumb and forefinger, he rolls it gently, sending sharp shocks of ecstasy down to my core.

The other hand slides between us, unerringly landing on my most sensitive spot. I moan a second time, much louder. My rhythm on his cock speeds up, as my body takes what it needs.

"Oh stars, oh Avirix," I gasp, unable to contain all of what I'm feeling in my skin alone. I'm driven higher, then higher still. I feel as hot as the sun and as luminous as the moon.

Dropping my head to Avirix's, I begin to kiss him while continuing to ride him. He devours my mouth, plundering it with his clever tongue. I'm half-sobbing from how good it feels, barely able to keep up my motions as my muscles start to go weak from bliss.

Of course, Avirix senses this. In one twist of his muscled torso, he flips us. The universe spins around me, rather pleasantly. When it rights itself, my love is on top of me, nestled deep between my legs.

Agonizingly, wonderfully slowly, he draws himself out of me, inch by inch. I whimper at the aching loss of him, before he plunges his shaft all the way back in at once.

I scream, the depth of his penetration sending a surge of new fire through me. He does it again, and again, each time forcing a sobbing wail of delirious delight from me.

Avirix thrusts into me like this until I think I can't take it anymore, I'll simply combust then and there. Right at my breaking point, he slows, finding just the right rhythm for both of us. I take in a ragged breath, letting the physical euphoria spread from its concentration at my core throughout my entire frame.

"I love you," he growls, lust thickening his already deep voice. "Shaper, Evalie, I never knew I could love anyone this much."

I'm wordless, too far gone to share my feelings with language. Avirix knows my emotions already, though. Instead I reach out and drag his head down to me, showing him exactly how much I love him with a passionate kiss.

Of all the ways we've pleasured each other this night, that is the one that pushes us over the edge.

Avirix moans into my mouth as my hips rise up greedily to meet him. He begins slamming into me, hard and fast. My body is ready, my walls grasping at him as he drives in and out.

His cock pulses into me, emptying his seed deep inside my heat. The throbbing might of him spurs me on, until my orgasm explodes through me like a supernova. I'm a blazing star, streaking through the heavens as I call out Avirix's name. He is the earth I fall to, shuddering as I cling to him.

My eyes are blurry with ecstasy, with love, with wonder. With gratitude, for the life I've found, and the fated bond that brought me there.

THIRTY-EIGHT

ZIW

The throbbing pulse of the Life Tree fills me as I walk the darkened steps of the monastery. My night time walks give me a chance to clear my mind and focus my soul, so that I may better hear the spirit of the planet.

Tonight, however, I have an agenda. I step into the moonlit garden of the monastery, and see a lone figure in the shadows.

"Hail Justan, of the Skuyr Mountain Clan Vargo," I say with a solemn respect for a fellow Reider.

"Hail Ziw, Mentor of Genesis," he responds. Then he lets slip a toothy grin. "You acknowledge me as Reider?"

"You are aware of the same teachings as I, Justan." I give the younger initiate a wry smile. "Any Skuyr who joins our ranks must do so in secret, and no one outside the order may know of it. Thus was laid down by Kor, Ehro, and Aelix."

"The Original Reiders," he whispers.

I nod.

"The original *zalshagri*."

"Dialects change," I say. "And while I believe it was

spoken differently in those days, it's the same type of bond."
I think of Avirix and Evalie, their faces glowing with love in
front of the Soul Tree. "It's good to see something as pure as
what they have, in these divided times. But -- I know you
have a question for me. Ask it."

"Do they know all that comes with the bond?" Justan
accepts my foreknowledge of his visit without a blink. "Do
they know the history behind it, and what the planet
expects? Do they know how it came to start or why they are
here?"

"They do not." I shake my head. "And they do not need
to know."

"Do you not feel it necessary to tell two *zalshagri*, who
found each other despite the schism between their peoples,
how their match came to be?"

I pause in my thoughts. My mind wanders to the original Drokan who began our order. We know of them as the
Wise Ones. The Original Reiders. Kor. Ehro. Aelix. Each of
whom found their human mates, just as King Avirix did.

I think about how they established our order. *Why* they
established our order. To keep the secrets of this planet. To
keep the secrets of the humans -- and their place in the
galaxy.

Some days, it is a crushing burden. This is one of those
days.

So, I look to the stars.

"From the stars they came," I say quietly.

"And to the stars we shall one day go, so that they may
come again," Justan finishes for me. "This is a simple phrase
taught to all novitiates in the order. It does not answer my
question."

I place my hand on Justan's shoulder. I know he wants
to know the deeper truth. He's clever and observant enough

to know it's there, but that isn't enough. He cannot learn this secret through hard study and devotion alone.

No.

The true nature of our world, and the galaxy, is a gift -- no, a burden -- reserved for a chosen few such as myself.

"We must not say anything for now." My voice is mild, but I speak with finality. "Krodo will act as he thinks is best."

My decision is enough for the Skuyr. He nods and walks away, our meeting concluded.

I look up again at the stars.

And pray that one day my burden is lifted.

THE END (FOR NOW). To read more about the daily lives of Avirix and Evalie join my newsletter to get a slice of life story at https://www.subscribepage.com/AthenaStorm.

To get a better understanding of the secrets Ziw is talking about, check out the preview after this!

PREVIEW

To begin to learn the secrets of the planet Genesis, check out the story, Alien Primal's Prize! A preview is included here!

PROLOGUE

The Story So Far...

THE YEAR IS 2338. Humanity has weathered it's infancy and has navigated to the stars. They've colonized other worlds and become a space faring civilization and formed the Interstellar Human Confederation.

Along the way, they've come to discover that the galaxy is actually a pretty crowded place. There are several political entities in the galaxy.

The Trident Alliance is composed of the Vakutan, the Pi'rell, and the Alzhon.

The Ataxian Coalition is composed of the Odex, Kreetu, Grolgath, and Shorcu.

The Coalition and the Alliance has been fighting a war for about 350 years. At its heart, it's an existential conflict that determines whether the known galaxy will be guided by the teachings of the Ataxian religion or by the capitalistic and technocratic tendencies of the Trident Alliance.

Details are unclear how the war between the Alliance and Coalition started, but atrocities in the name of protecting the innocent have been committed by both sides.

Several races, trying to remain neutral and unaffiliated with either side have formed a loose political union known as the League of Non-Aligned Races. Each race maintains their sovereignty. Member states meet infrequently to discuss trade and security matters, but no true leadership exists.

Many races over the centuries have settled and created a political entity known as the Helios Combine, situated between Coalition and Alliance space and next to the Badlands - a region of space with many stellar phenomena. The Combine is known for it's slave based economy, its capitalist based caste system, and a rigid social class system.

Humanity had for a long time maintained their neutrality, but after multiple encounters, sided with the Alliance in their war against the Coalition.

In a galaxy that's ripped apart by war, the only light is that one day, a measure of hope will be given to the hopeless.

That day has yet to come...

THIRTY-NINE

CRESS

"Cressida Porter, you're done for the day."

"I'm not finished." I wipe the sweat from my brow and reach for the wrench once more. This isn't a hard task. Simple maintenance on one of the air-cooling systems, a luxury on a voyage such as ours. I should be able to do this.

"Yes, you are." Officer Moira bites the inside of her cheek. "You're doing more harm than good there."

"I've almost got it."

"No, you haven't. Haven't you had any mechanical training?"

"No," I frown.

"Then why are you fiddling with the cooling systems?"

"Because you assigned the tasks," I sigh.

"How am I supposed to know the qualifications of each and every one of you? Unless you have *doctor* or some kind of science job next to your name, I know nothing."

There wouldn't be anything like that next to my name. There are exactly one thousand people aboard *The*

Precursor. My guess is at least half of them come from a useful background. The rest of us were volunteers.

What else are you supposed to do when you're heading out past the League of Non Aligned Races and into uncharted space.

"How am I supposed to learn if I'm not allowed to finish my tasks to completion?" I ask.

"What are you trying to learn for?" Moira looks me up and down. "You're not going to the new colony with a profession. You're essentially a breeder."

I clench my jaw.

"I'm no such thing."

"Whatever you say. Clock off for the night. I'll try to assign you to work with someone more experienced next time."

I'm not a damn breeder. I volunteered for this excursion because there's nothing left for me anywhere else. We set off from Novaria yesterday. Maybe it was the day before last. It's hard to keep track of time passing when there's no sunrise or sunset. It's still strange for me to wake up in the morning only to look out the window and see nothing but black pinpricked with stars.

The Precursor is a huge, slow-moving spacecraft that's expected to make at least half a dozen stops before we enter the barren stretch to get to the farthest reaches of the galaxy.

The ship, named for the mythical Precursors that some races believe came before any other life on the galaxy can only maintain superluminal speed for so long. We have stops scheduled along the way to bring on more passengers, trade for supplies, and then prepare ourselves for the final voyage out into uncharted space.

Advanced Colonization Directives, or ACD, the Trident Alliance based corporation that is running this operation has discovered some colonies out beyond League and Coalition space.

It wasn't long before the Interstellar Human Confederation contracted out ACD to run a colonization mission out into some of the newly discovered systems.

Human colonists were needed – and the way it works with each of these expeditions is that the company comes out to various IHC and Alliance worlds, looking for humans.

There's usually a free dinner followed by a presentation. You get a signing bonus for agreeing to pack up your life and go look for opportunity without all the creature comforts of the holonet, sonic showers, and living amongst trillions of sapient beings in your corner of the galaxy.

But despite whatever you might lose, there was one big thing that made colonization more attractive than anything.

Getting away from the fucking war.

Every day it seemed that the various powers in the galaxy were hellbent on destroying one another. If it wasn't an IHC colony world getting overrun then it was a massive space battle between the Alliance and Coalition. Or Reapers attacking.

It wasn't hard to imagine society just crumbling all around us. The entire galaxy going mad.

I wanted to get away from the frying pan before it burst into fire.

I wanted to spend the rest of my life not having to worry about who out of my companions or family was going to die next.

So, I went to the dinner.

I ate my free food, listened to the presentation, and signed my name.

The goal was to colonize and defend one of the habitable planets in the Outer Rim, past the League of Non Aligned Races. The Captain estimated it would take us around six months to make that journey.

Up until now, I've avoided space travel. With both parents dead and gone and all of my brother's killed in combat against the Coalition, there's nothing left for me to stick around for. I need a fresh start. A new colony is taking that need to the extreme, but hey, whatever works.

I leave the cooling unit to a qualified professional and sign my timesheet. Everyone on board gets a chance to earn a little extra income. It's a way to jump-start the economy on whatever planet we end up settling. The powers that be who've approved this mission have provided funds for all the necessities, however, pocket change isn't a necessity. I should've realized all of the jobs would require some kind of specialized skill.

I'm average at just about everything. That's not a bad thing, in my opinion. I can manage everything that's thrown at me, except tuning up a cooling unit. I'm fair at gardening, coding, first aid, and all manner of useful skills. I'm just not the best. The best are the ones who get the jobs. If I'd had known how things work ahead of time, I would've taken a course or something.

I make my way through the labyrinth of the ship. I get lost three times before finding the mess hall. *The Precursor* has three, but I prefer to use the one closest to my quarters. It minimizes the chance of getting lost. I'm sure I'll master the layout eventually, though it may be time to disembark by the time I do so.

"Cress!" Merrit, my bunkmate and the closest thing I have to a friend on the ship waves me over. I grab a tray and pile it with food before joining them. The Captain warned us to enjoy the food while we have it. There's a good chance we'll be moved to rations before we make it to the Outer Rim. Once that happens, the next time we'll have a normal meal depends on how long it takes us to grow it.

A lot of attention in the galaxy is spent focusing on who is colonizing in The Frontier. That's the area of space that's bordered by the Trident Alliance, the Interstellar Human Confederation, and the League of Non Aligned Races.

But what doesn't get as much mention is the Outer Rim. Past the farthest of planets that belong to the League, it's bordered by a sliver of the IHC, the Helios Combine, and the Ataxian Coalition.

It's much quieter and more peaceful, unlike the swash-buckling, anything goes, hypercapitalistic atmosphere of The Frontier.

Still, through their open borders agreements with the Helios Combine (for a price) and the IHC, the Alliance manages to send some ships to the Outer Rim.

And where there are Alliance ships, there's bound to be Coalition craft – looking for a fight.

Thankfully, we've seen none so far.

But every time we mention the Outer Rim, I wonder if we'll make it there in one piece.

There is a level on *The Precursor* dedicated to agriculture, but the crops planted are not yet seedlings. It was too risky to bring grown plants and attempt to transfer them. We need as many healthy, living plants as possible.

Sitting at the table with Merrit are several other women I've come to know over the last day or so. I suspect we'll become friends eventually. We're too busy getting our bearings to focus on friendship right now.

"You're late," Rosalie says with a sly smile.

"I wasn't aware I ate on a schedule," I reply with a grin as I take my seat.

"You're not, but you've missed all of the good gossip," she shrugs.

"We've only been on this ship for two days, if that. How can there be gossip?"

"We've been on this ship for forty-two hours now," Merrit says matter-of-factly. "That's plenty of time for gossip to generate."

"Lay it on me," I nod.

"Vianne has a lover."

"I do not!" Vianne protests. "I simply think Corporal Reddinbaker likes me."

"And do you like him?"

Vianne levels Merrit with a blank look.

"Have you seen Corporal Reddinbaker? He looks like a bloated fish."

I slap my hand over my mouth to keep from laughing.

"That's not very nice," Rosalie sniffs.

"Neither is he," Vianne scowls.

"Is that the only gossip worth sharing?" I say in an attempt to steer the conversation to a less prickly topic.

"No. Forty-two hours and we're already bored out of our skulls," Merrit sighs. "I hope we get some excitement soon.

"Officer Moira called me a breeder today. That's sort of interesting," I offer.

"It's not interesting, it's downright bitchy. What's her problem?"

"She hoped to move up in rank when she signed on," Rosalie replies. "She's bitter about remaining an officer."

"That's no reason to call me a breeder," I huff. "I didn't sign on to birth the next generation. And I'm not a Companion or any other sort of prostitute. And the last I checked, the IHC was running this colonization. Not the Helios Combine where slavery is still legal."

"We're going to need a stable population base," Vianne counters.

"True, but that wasn't what I signed on for," I reply.

"But are you averse to it?" Vianne asks.

"No," I shake my head. "But I'd like to do it when I'm ready with the right person, not because a colony is at risk of inbreeding. We have plenty of people to prevent that. Breeders aren't necessary."

"I dare her to say something like that to me," Merit murmurs.

"Don't go making a bad name for yourself before our first week is up,' Rosalie cautions with a smile. "I'm sure the Captain will have no problem leaving you at our first stop."

"He'll have to find me first," Merit grins. "This is a big ship. There are plenty of places to hide."

I roll my eyes and finish my last bite of food.

"I'm going to turn in for the night, ladies," I say with a smile. "See you tomorrow?"

"Don't be late," Rosalie says.

"I'll come with you." Merit pushes away from the table. "I'm planning to get up extra early to snag a good job."

"You're an engineer. Shouldn't all the jobs open to you be good?" I ask.

"We haven't been *en voyage* long enough for *The Precursor* to need any engineering work," she shrugs. "I won't be useful until we hit that final stretch to the Outer

Rim. Until then, it's toilet cleaning and dishwashing for me."

We make our way back to our room. One thing I've noticed about Merrit is that she can fall asleep in just over a minute. I'm not that lucky. Best case scenario, it takes me an hour to fall asleep. Since *The Precursor* is a new place, it's been taking me longer. Tonight is no exception.

I toss and turn, unable to keep my eyes closed for more than a few minutes at a time. I want to get up and wander the ship but I don't want anyone asking questions. *The Precursor* doesn't yet feel like home enough for me to stroll freely like that.

Suddenly, the ship lurches so violently that I'm thrown against the wall our bunk is pressed against.

"What the fuck?" Merrit groans.

The Precursor lurches again, this time in the opposite direction. I'm flung from the top bunk and land hard on the floor.

"What's going on?" I cry.

Before Merrit can answer, the emergency alarm blares throughout the ship, drowning out all other noise.

"We have to get to a safe-room," Merrit screams over the squeal of the sirens.

We stumble out of the room together. Dozens of people pour into the corridors, all scrambling for a safe-room. Merrit and I find one, but it's already stuffed to the gills. There's no room for us. The next one we reach is shut and locked. Horrified faces of those lucky enough to make it inside peer out at us through the small viewport.

"Go to the port side," Merrit tells me. "I'll go starboard. We'll have better luck if we split up."

I nod and run hell for leather toward the opposite side

of the ship. Many run with me. It dawns on me that there might not be enough safe-rooms to hold us all.

I pass by a panel of windows. The view outside stops me in my tracks. There are ships all around us. I recognize the mark of the Alliance on some of them. The rest are dark ships of the Coalition. We must've drifted right into a battle by mistake.

The Precursor isn't a war vessel. It's neither speedy nor streamlined. The navigation team must be trying their hardest to bring her around before she takes on any damage. Merrit might be getting a job after all.

The sky fills with fire as explosions go off between the stars. This isn't just a skirmish. This is as bad as it gets.

Blinding white light eats away at the blackness of space but before I can determine its source, another explosion goes off, much closer to us this time. It's powerful enough to tip *The Precursor*.

I can't linger any longer. A third explosion, more violent than the first two combined, sends a shockwave rippling through space. It tears through the war vessels nearest to it. I have to get somewhere safe before it strikes *The Precursor*.

I realize I'm alone in the corridors. All of the safe-rooms in sight are locked up.

I duck into the nearest room. It's nothing more than a storage closet. I spy a long, metal box that would ordinarily be used for storing weapons but has been repurposed for the farming supplies we'll eventually need. I throw the supplies out and climb in. Looking up from my back, the box eerily resembles a coffin.

I shake the thought away and pull the box shut. The latches automatically click into place.

The shockwave hits, or I assume it does. I'm thrown against the side of the box. The box slams into the wall.

Somehow, I'm tumbling and floating all at once. My bones bark in protest as they're slammed into the sides of the box again and again. My head strikes the reinforced siding hard. I'm slammed by something outside the box.

I can't help but scream. I keep screaming, through the pain, through the uncertainty, and through the fear. I scream until everything goes black.

FORTY

KOR

C lear skies. Slight breeze. Too much sun. Even my experienced eyes are reduced to squinting through its gleam.

I smell the Galvains before I see them, which is impressive since they're twice the size of our tents.

We move low through the high grass, using it to our advantage.

"We'll take the herd from the north."

I stop dead in my tracks and turn around to face the horned Drokan male who had the nerve to bark orders at the hunting pack. I'm the pack leader. I give the orders. Anyone who dares give an order to my pack is challenging my authority. I can't allow that.

"What was that, Martok?"

"We'll take them from the north." He stared into my eyes as he spoke. This was a direct challenge.

I stand up to my full height. My shoulders and chest are now visible above the tall grass. If there are any Galvains nearby, they will spot me but that's no longer my concern. Martok needs to be put back in his place.

"You and what hunting pack?" I shoot glares as the hunters around me. If two or three stand with Martok, this will be more complicated than I anticipated. The other hunters have no reason to doubt my ability to lead them. I've been the leader of the Open Plains Hunters for the last ten years. I took the honor the day I came of age. I out-hunted and out-killed everyone else who had a stake to the claim.

Martok hasn't even been with the hunters for five years.

None of my hunters stepped up to share Martok's claim. A feral grin spreads across my mouth. I bare my teeth, ready to sink them into his throat if need be.

"Still think you're going north?"

"I think you're getting on in your age. It's time you let the young ones take over," he shrugs. I'm not sure if he understands that he's alone in this or if he doesn't care. Bravery is an admirable trait. Foolishness and recklessness aren't. Neither do the pack any good.

I bark out a laugh. I'm nowhere near old age. I'm in my prime and will stay in my prime for another decade yet. One day, I will step down at the leader of the Plains hunters but that day will not come for some time. When it does, it sure as hell won't be Martok who takes the mantle from me.

"You're young and inexperienced," I snarl. "Stay in the back of the pack like the whelp you are and I will not grind your horns into dust for your transgression."

"Over my dead body." Martok leans forward, taking up a fighting stance.

"As you wish." I lunge at him, tackling him to the ground. It's not difficult to get the upper-hand. I take him by the horns and drag him through the grass. He fights against me but I'm much stronger. He should've known better.

Whenever he starts to struggle into a standing position, I knock him back down. I yank him forward and press my knee into his back, forcing him to lay on his stomach on the dirt. I still have him by the horns. Like mine, they are light brown and twist up before bending back over his skull. I grab the tip of one horn and apply pressure.

"You know I can break this if I want to, right?" I hiss. "Do you know what happens when a Drokan breaks a horn?"

Martok writhes beneath me but it's no use. He's trapped until I allow him to move freely.

"It never grows back," I continue. "Would you like me to rearrange your horns for you?"

Before Martok can manage a response, a deafening boom cracks through the air. The ground beneath my feet trembles. The sun grows brighter and brighter until I can see nothing else. I shield my eyes until they adjust to the brightness. Only then do I realize it's not the sun getting brighter, it's something else.

It looks as if the sky has been torn open. Something spills through. It's bigger than anything that's ever graced our skies. It's the size of a small mountain, but it's not made of rock and stone. There is no grass or greenery on it. It cannot be natural.

Its body is made of something shiny. It reflects the sun down onto us. Fire spills from its insides. If it's some kind of great sky-beast, it's been seriously injured. Its sides are peppered with holes and gashed, though no blood or innards drip out.

Pieces of its hide clatter to the earth but it's like no hide I've ever seen before. It's not flexible or malleable. It falls in rigid sheets and slices the earth where it hits

I allow Martok to get to his feet in case we need to run.

"What is that?" My right-hand hunter, Calbrin, shouts.

I don't have an answer for him. I have no idea what this is.

"Where is it going?" Another hunter asks.

Something different falls from the flaming beast as it drifts over the Plains. It's not a sheet of hide. It's thicker, like some kind of box. Its fall is not very long but it lands with a solid thud.

"Will it hit the Center?"

A pit forms in my stomach at the thought. The Center is the heart and soul of the Drokan. If the Center is lost, so are we.

"Get to the Center," I order. "Ensure Chief Tahakan is protected."

"What about you?" Calbrin asks.

My gaze drifts back to the box. I can't explain it, but something is pulling me toward it. I have to know what it is before I do anything else. Blood thrums in my ears. My breath comes in ragged drags.

"I will investigate on my own then meet you there," I say.

I turn my gaze back to the flaming beast. It clears the Center and drifts over the peaks of the Snowy Mountains. The belly of the beast grazes the peak of the tallest mountain, crushing the peak to dust. No doubt it will cause an avalanche. The Drokan who reside there will have to flee.

"Go!" I bark to Calbrin.

He doesn't argue. He gathers the hunters and they quickly set off in the direction of the Center. I make my way toward the box.

I approach it slowly, jabbing at it with my spear to make sure it isn't rigged to attack or burst into flames like the beast that dropped it. Could it be an egg or some sort? It doesn't look like any egg I've ever seen.

I run my hand along its surface. It's perfectly smooth. Smoother than a river rock. It's not living. It's scalding hot, likely from the flames it was surrounded by, yet it's not burned. There are two separate parts of this box but they're fused together. I can't pry it open. There's something holding the two components together, but it's been damaged by the heat. I can't use it to open the box.

My hands burn, but not badly enough to make me stop. I have to know what's inside. I don't even know *how* I know something's inside. I just do. Every fiber of my being grows more and more desperate to open the box. I don't understand it. I've never felt anything like this before. I feel like a rabid Watgrat from the Dark Forest. Those creatures will stop at nothing to obtain what they're after. They've been known to claw through stone if they feel the need.

I glance at my talons thoughtfully. The box is strong, but it's not solid. Perhaps, I can be like the Watgrat and burrow through the surface.

I run my talon along the seal, gently slipping it between the two fused pieces. Luckily, it's not fused all the way around. I slide my talons deeper, forcing a gap between the two pieces of the box to appear. Whatever the box is made of isn't as strong as stone, but it's close. It takes all of my strength to force the pieces apart.

The top of the box flies off with a hard snap. There are deep welts across my fingertips. It's a wonder I didn't break a talon though that wouldn't have been the worst thing to happen. Unlike our horns, a talon will grow back.

I'm not prepared for what's in the box. A female lies with her limbs bent at a strange angle. She looks like me in some ways, but vastly different in others. She has two arms and two legs like I do, though she's smaller than any female Drokan I've ever met. Her long, dark hair frames her face. Her skin is pale but not pale enough to be of the Snowy Mountain Drokan. She has no talons, ridges, or horns.

I feel a tug deep inside me, stronger and more insistent than the tug that pulled me to the box in the first place. My heart races. My breath catches in my chest. It feels like the world is being pulled out from under me yet falling into place all at once. I only know of one thing that's meant to feel this way. This couldn't possibly be it.

I've heard older Drokan describe feelings similar to what I'm feeling now. They felt it when they first set eyes on their mate.

Nothing compares to seeing one's mate for the first time. I wouldn't know personally. I'm not mated. Drokan storytellers spend hours trying to describe the sensation of finding a mate. From what they say, it feels like what I'm feeling now.

There is a word that our storytellers have used in the past.

Jalshagar.

Fated one. Fated mate.

The one that you know you will spend the rest of your days with. The one who will care for you. The one you will protect and worship as they worship you.

The one who will bring you pleasure.

The one who will please you.

That can't be what I feel. The small, unconscious female in a box discarded from a flaming sky leviathan cannot be my mate.

That's impossible.

. . .

TO BE CONTINUED. To keep reading please look for Alien Primal's Mate.

BOOKS OF THE ATHENAVERSE

Intergalactic Fated Mates:

Nanny For the Alien King

Maid For Him

Reaper's Property:

Monster

Savage

Brute

'90s Nostalgia Fated Mates

My Boyfriend Is An Alien

My Hero is An Alien

My Neighbor Is An Alien

Reaper's Pet Series (An Athenaverse Collaboration with Zora Black):

Caged Mate

Caged Prey

Caged Toy

Caged Slayer

Caged Property

Caged Pearl

Caged Beauty

Caged Bride

Bride to Beasts Series:

Zuvok

Zerberu

Vyker

Maru

Gorn

Kurg

Soldiers of Hope Series:

Hope In A Time Of War

Love In A Time of Sorrow

Faith In A Time of Fury

Marauder Mates Series:

Sorta Seized By The Alien

Totally Taken By The Alien

Untamed

Beauty and The Alien

Jave

Conquered Mates (An Athenaverse Collaboration with Tara Starr):

Warlord's Property

Alpha's Prey

Brute's Challenge

Alien Torturer's Pet

Alien Savage's Doll